I0822308

to
my grandmother,
for telling the stories;

my mother,
for helping me remember;

and my children,
for listening.

Heather Daughrity

Published by Parlor Ghost Press, an imprint of Watertower Hill Publishing, LLC

www.parlorghostpress.com
www.watertowerhill.com

Cover and internal artwork by Susan Roddey at The Snark Shop by Fairie & Fae

Internal Formatting by J.L. Daughrity, The Watertower Hill Publishing Company

Cover photo credits: Brice McVicar / Shadow and Light Photography

Printed in the United States of America
10 9 8 7 6 5 4 3 2

Library of Congress Control Number: 2023114774
ISBN: 979-8-9893011-6-4

Also by Heather Daughrity

Anthologies

House of Haunts

Novels

Knock Knock

Tales My Grandmother Told Me

Echoes of the Dead: Collected Hauntings

Anthology Contributions (as Heather Miller)

These Lingering Shadows

The Horror Zine Magazine Fall, 2022

Into the Forest: Tales of the Baba Yaga

Tales from the Monoverse

Head Blown: Extreme Horror Stories

The Depths Unleashed, Volume One

The Horror Collection: Creature Feature Edition

Anthology Contributions (as Heather Daughrity)

Deathrealm: Spirits

The Monsters Next Door

Table of Contents

FOREWORD

by Ronald Kelly

When Heather Daughrity mentioned the title of this collection of stories, I was intrigued. When she told me how and why it was inspired, I knew I had to read it. After I read her introduction, I knew I would probably enjoy it. At that point in time, however, I had no idea that I would end up loving this book so very much.

When you have been in the writing business as long as I have, you happen across plenty of writers who make up stories in their head and present them in an engaging and professional manner. But you also come across a rare few who seem to be hardwired with a natural talent and a fluidity of prose that cannot be gleaned from creative writing classes or mentor-taught retreats. Their method and motive for relaying fiction or non-fiction is practically infused into their being, as much a part of them as muscle and bone.

I refer to these writers as "storytellers" in the purest sense of the word. Whenever I come across one, I usually reach the realization that what they possess is almost of a hereditary nature. Because nine times out of ten, someone in their family – someone they loved and held a very special connection to – was a storyteller themself.

Given my personal history, I consider myself of that fraternity and, after reading this book, I know, without a doubt, that Heather is, too.

Heather's Grandma Nan was very much like my own Grandmama Clara. Their lives were so similar, in personal experience as well as character and spirit, that they could have very well been sisters. And both had a flair and desire to spin yarns and tell tales, be it family history, ghost stories, or anecdotal accounts of life in general… joys and heartaches, triumphs as well as hardships.

Like Heather, I grew up listening to my grandmother's stories. When other boys my age were out playing baseball or riding bikes, I was content to sit on the front porch on a warm summer day or before the potbelly stove in the kitchen on a cold winter's night and simply listen… and absorb.

Grandmama's words were as captivating and entertaining as *Charlotte's Web* or *Where the Red Fern Grows*, or later in my teenage years, *To Kill a Mockingbird*. And just as Heather, when it came time to try my hand at writing and spinning my own tales, I drew from the familial well that was so satisfying and plentiful. Many of my stories of Southern rural horror sprang from the same ones that crossed Grandmama's lips: The tale of the little girl who drank from a creek, swallowed a snake, and carried it inside her into adulthood (*Miss Abigail's Delicate Condition*), the crazed handyman with the withered hand that terrified her during her early childhood (*Midnight Grinding),* and the loss of a beloved doll when her playhouse in the depths of a hidden cave was sealed shut with an avalanche of earth and rock… and how it could have easily been her tomb, if she had been playing there that day (*The China Doll*).

So, you see, I owe Grandmama a lot, for awakening that spark – that *hunger* – to share my own style of storytelling, not vocally, but through the written word. Reading these tales that Heather has penned and collected into a single volume, it is clear to see that Grandma Nan had the same lasting and transformative effect on her as well.

As you begin to read *Tales My Grandmother Told Me,* I suggest that you to approach these sixteen unsettling stories in two different ways.

First, as tales crafted by a relatively new, but genuinely gifted storyteller; one who can convey a variety of emotions quite effectively…

sometimes tenderly with a velvet touch, while at other times like a cold shiver down the length of your spine in the dead of night.

And, secondly, experience them as connective links between two generations: one adept at telling tales orally, the other through the magic of the keyboard and the printed page. Undeniably, it makes for a loving and complementary melding of two distinct, but individual, narrative forms.

Like I said before, I cherish this book for what it has to offer; the places it has taken me – comforting or unpleasant – and the folks it has introduced me to – good or bad. I feel privileged to have had the opportunity to have read it before publication. You, dear readers… you have the added pleasure of holding it in your hands. To feel its solidity, to live and breathe through the conduit between the printed word and your own imagination.

Somewhere, in that distant place where storytellers of past generations spend eternity, I like to imagine Nan and Clara sitting on some heavenly front porch, shelling beans and telling tales, playfully trying to outshine one another. Blissful in the knowledge that their grandkids carry on the tradition that they, themselves, had a hand in conjuring.

Ronald Kelly
Brush Creek, Tennessee
June 2022

Introduction

My grandmother was a character. Born on the cusp of the Great Depression, raised in a two-room house with two brothers and two sisters, and coming of age during World War II, she lived a life that most of us today can only read about.

She was the second of her parents' five children, christened with the most awful name they could come up with, one which I can only safely reveal to you now because she's not here to smack me if I say it: Cleatus Gleneva.

Yes, you read that right. A tiny, precious little baby girl named CLEATUS GLENEVA. As you can imagine, she hated this name and quickly took on the simple and somewhat prettier nickname of "Nan," and that is the name she would be known by for the rest of her life. Nan West who became Nan Morrow who became Nan Ubieta.

To me, she was Grandma Nan, to those of my children who are old enough to have known her, she was Nana.

Grandma Nan was all of four-feet-eleven-and-a-half-inches tall (and the half was very important). She was scrawny when young, pleasantly plump by the time I knew her. Pictures of her as a young woman show black hair and a determined countenance. By the time I came along, her hair was silvery-white and she was more likely to laugh than to scowl.

She was easily the smartest person I know, in spite of never finishing high school. You've heard that expression "a mind like a sponge"? That is exactly what she had. The most wonderful thing about her was that if she didn't know the answer to a question, she'd say, "Well, let's find out!" Nothing stopped her.

My grandmother was also quite the stickler for proper spelling, punctuation, and grammar. She made sure that I knew how to both speak and write properly, correcting me gently when I made a mistake. Her great pet peeve was the use of the qualifier "very" when it made no sense. Someone saying "very pregnant" was enough to send her into a tirade: "You can't be very pregnant. You can't be barely pregnant. There are no varying degrees of pregnancy. You either are or you aren't."

I'd laugh at her of course, but anyone who knows me will see that this is exactly where I get it from.

The brief synopsis of my grandmother's life is thus: she was born in 1929, raised by parents who worked the cotton fields; they were poor but they didn't know it, because everyone around them was, too. She left school at the end of her junior year to marry my grandfather, newly returned from a war just ended.

Over the next eight years, she would be pregnant seven times: four miscarriages, one stillbirth, and two healthy babies: my uncle in 1947 and my mother in 1954. She was so tiny, my grandmother, that carrying a baby was a great strain on her body. But she wanted her boy and her girl, and she got them.

Her story at this point, unfortunately, shifts into one so common to housewives in the mid-twentieth-century: my grandmother, like so many other women in her position, was prescribed anti-anxiety and anti-depression medications to help her deal with the reality that was her life. In 1959, when my mother was five years old, my grandparents divorced.

My grandmother remarried in 1963, this time to a man as completely opposite my grandfather as you can imagine. Joe was kind, quiet, and gentle. He loved my grandmother with a devotion that she could not quite return. She cared for him, she appreciated him, but I don't think she was ever truly in love with him. He provided a steady home and a steady income to help support her children, and he loved those children, and eventually their children, too, as if they were his own. Joe died when I was four years old, so my memories of him are few and faded, but I do remember that he was always kind, and that he would do anything for my grandmother.

After Joe died in 1985, my grandmother moved in with us. For most of my childhood and adolescent years, she lived with us, and we became very close. I can remember coming home after half-day kindergarten and sitting in the living room with her, tomato soup and a grilled cheese sandwich on a TV tray, watching *The Birds* or *The Uninvited* or *The Exorcist*. She loved scary movies, so I loved them, too.

When I was around eleven years old, I started helping myself to her bookshelf, and I discovered the wonders of Edgar Allan Poe, Guy de Maupassant, and all the Victorian writers who penned the ghost stories collected in the anthologies she loved.

We watched movies, and we read books, and we discussed them, but that wasn't all in my grandmother's macabre arsenal.

That woman had stories, and that is what this book is about.

Our family hails, in distant ages, mostly from Ireland and Scotland; in the more recent past, from the misty hills and hollers of the Ozark Mountains. Whether centuries or decades ago, we come from an imaginative, creative, superstitious lot who made their home in places full of magic and mystery. We are storytellers and always have been.

Most of the stories in this collection are based on tales my grandmother told. She'd tell them as bedtime stories, or on dark autumn nights while the wind howled around the house. She told them at Halloween parties and on long car trips. Any time she had a captive audience, she told these stories, complete with terrifying voices, creepy wailings, awful facial expressions, and whatever sound effects she could create with the objects at hand.

Of the sixteen stories in this book, ten are based on my grandmother's stories. Three more are based on old songs she used to sing. The remaining three are a story about my grandfather's house, a boogeyman made up by one of my older children to scare the younger ones, and a tale that comes from my own life.

I have added to the basic plots, embellishing a bit, filling in details to take them from five-minute tales to five-thousand-word stories. I have endeavored to take them from spooky to scary while still maintaining that feeling that you get when listening to a tale around a campfire, that feeling which is a mixture of fear and fun. Some stories are darker than others. Some contain supernatural elements, some are purely the evil that man inflicts on man. A few of the stories are based on true events, others are clearly completely made up. At the back of the book, in the Author's Notes, you'll find a little information about the origins of each one.

I hope you enjoy the stories you're about to read. Grandma Nan died in 2006, just shy of her seventy-seventh birthday. I hope she's smiling proudly from heaven, with a little glint of impish delight in her eye, as this book goes out into the world.

CG "Nan" Ubieta, circa 1940s

VICE

"She won't tell you," Roger said, flicking the ash from his cigarette into the grass.

Chelsea watched it glow orange for a moment and then fade into nothingness. She did not look up. She hoped Roger wouldn't say any more, hoped the group would pass her by without pressuring her to take part in this little game.

She really hadn't wanted to come in the first place, but Roger had begged her and she hadn't had the heart to tell him no. Now she found herself in the woods, in the dark, circling a campfire with people she barely knew. Inevitably, as night had settled around them, the ghost stories had begun.

"She won't tell you," he said again, after a long drag and an even longer exhale, "but she has a great story. I know. She's told it to me. But she's scared of it. The thing in the story. So she doesn't like to talk about it."

Chelsea glared at the ground. She did not want to meet Roger's eyes. She had told him that story in strictest confidence. She should have known better than to trust him with it.

But now the whole group was interested, curious. What *thing,* they wanted to know. What was the story about, what kind of creature scared her so much?

Chelsea raised her eyes, defiant, and stared directly at Roger. She avoided letting her eyes wander to the shadows that danced and twisted around him in the firelight.

"Fine," she said. "I'll tell it."

Cheers erupted from the other campers, and Chelsea waited to speak until they had quieted down.

The forest was abuzz with noise around them, insects and frogs and the occasional call of an owl. The fire burned low, smoldering in its ring of stones, quietly shifting and popping.

Chelsea hunched forward, elbows on her knees, hands hanging limp between her legs. She spoke just loudly enough to be heard over the background noise.

"This story is true," she began. "It was told to me by my grandmother, Loretta, a story of real things that happened to her. When she was younger, much younger, probably the same age we are now, she worked as a receptionist in a doctor's office.

"The doctor – Dr. Bailey – was a pulmonologist – a doctor who specialized in diseases of the lungs."

Around the firepit, the others leaned in, listening closely as Chelsea told her tale…

Day after day, she sat at her desk, signing people in, taking their payments. Day after day, she listened to them coughing and wheezing. She emptied waste baskets full of bloodied tissues and cleaned up the vomit when a coughing fit became more than just a cough.

The work was hard, physically hard at times and emotionally hard always. These were people who were dying, some slowly, some hurtling fast toward that final day, but all on the way and resigned to it. It was heartbreaking, and depressing. But the pay was good, and she had two kids at home and a husband who had run off with a barmaid, so Loretta stuck it out.

Every day at five o'clock, she tidied the office, said good-bye to the doctor, and went home to her children. She performed this job, just like this, every day for three years.

Then one day, the doctor asked her if she'd be willing to stay late a couple of days each week. He had patients who had a difficult time making it to appointments in the daytime due to their jobs and was considering extended office hours to accommodate them. It would mean more money, and her kids were old enough now to fend for themselves for a few extra hours, so she agreed.

The new office hours started the first week in October. Two more hours in the evening meant four additional patients. Loretta sat at her desk, listening as the building in which the office was located closed down around them.

By six o'clock, she'd admitted two patients, noted when the elevator stopped running and the lobby doors stopped opening; the various people who normally made a buzz of life in the rooms around them were gone, the building quiet. Out the one window in the waiting room, she watched as the golden blush of the afternoon faded to twilight and then the world outside was obscured by night. Two small lamps, one on her desk and one on a corner table, lent the room a dim amber glow.

From the back office, she could hear the low murmur of Dr. Bailey's voice and the occasional wracking cough from the patient. She looked down at the file in front of her to remind herself of the patient's name: George Harkin. Peeking inside, she scanned his intake chart. Stage three lung cancer.

As the sound of footsteps approached the door to the inner office, she quickly closed the file and put it away.

"Loretta here will get you set up with your next appointment, George."

Dr. Bailey smiled kindly at his patient. He always smiled kindly at everyone. Loretta wondered if he ever stopped smiling. It made her cheeks hurt just thinking about it. Dr. Bailey gave her a nod and went back into the exam area, the door clicking shut behind him.

The patient – George – attempted to smile at Loretta. It looked forced, painful, more grimace than grin. He was a middle-aged man, utterly plain in every way.

There was nothing remarkable or memorable about him, except the sound of the cough that erupted from him now. He turned his head, hacking into his balled-up fist. Loretta handed him a tissue. His eyes were red and bulging, tears running down his cheeks by the time he finished. She directed him to the wastebasket near the window.

That's when she saw it. As George turned his back and walked away from her to throw away his crumpled tissue, the shadows *moved.* Just behind him, following close on his heels, the shadows of the waiting room chairs seemed to pull toward him, a low mass of darkness that dogged his footsteps.

Loretta blinked her eyes a few times, looked again. George had already turned and was headed back to her. She craned her head, trying to see behind him. Were her eyes playing tricks on her? It did seem darker now in the rest of the room, behind him.

"Are you OK, miss?" he asked, and she gasped and sat back rigidly in her chair. Looking up into his face, the light seemed to come back into the room.

She gave a nervous laugh. “Just tired, I guess. Now, George, let’s get you set up for your next appointment.”

Two weeks later, George was back. Loretta watched him closely, and sure enough, as he sat in the waiting room wheezing, the darkness in the room seemed to draw toward him. He appeared oblivious, staring at the magazine in his hand like nothing was wrong.

Loretta busied herself with her end-of-the-day work, but her eyes kept darting back to George as the far end of the room grew darker around him, a pool of shadow gathering at his feet.

A sharp intake of breath made her glance up quickly from her typing.

George was holding his chest and gasping, but Loretta couldn't stop looking at the shadows.

A long arm of darkness was reaching up from the swirling mass at his feet, the impossible shape of a head and shoulders emerging as it pulled itself up his legs.

George's wheezing turned to a coughing fit and his face grew darker as he struggled for breath.

Loretta's mouth opened and closed, a scream trapped inside her as she pushed herself back from the desk, further away from the shadow.

Dr. Bailey rushed into the room, hurrying over to George. He stepped directly into the moving shadows like they weren't even there and began speaking quietly and soothingly to his patient, calming him down and pressing his stethoscope to the man's chest at the same time. As the wheezing and coughing began to ebb, the shadow shrunk back into itself until it was just a darkened spot on the carpet beneath George's chair once more.

"Loretta!" The doctor spoke firmly. "Call an ambulance. He needs the hospital."

She did as she was told, and a few minutes later an approaching siren heralded the arrival of the paramedics. George was helped onto a stretcher and carried out. Dr. Bailey went with them, and Loretta, not wanting to be left alone in the darkening room, rushed to follow.

In the back of the ambulance, one of the uniformed men was placing a mask over George's face, and as Loretta's eyes followed the attached tube down to its connected tank of oxygen, she saw the shadows of the street slip and slither into the floor beneath George's stretcher.

After a few words with Dr. Bailey, the ambulance men closed the doors on the back of their truck and set off toward the nearby hospital. Loretta watched until they were out of sight. Dr. Bailey guided her gently back into the office to gather her things and then told her to head home early.

When she stopped in the powder room on her way out, she could see why he'd let her leave. She was pale as a ghost and shaking all over. What had she seen? Had it been real? Was she going crazy?

November came and went. The weather grew colder, wetter, drearier. George remained in the hospital, and though she typed up Dr. Bailey's notes on his case after his visits to George, Loretta didn't see him again herself until the first week of December.

During a slow day in the office, Dr. Bailey came out to chat with her.

"I've been thinking, Loretta. Christmastime is upon us, and our patients up at the hospital could use a bit of holiday cheer. What do you think about making some visits, bringing along a few small gifts, trying to make their dark days a little lighter?"

How could she say no to that?

A few days later, she accompanied Dr. Bailey to the hospital. The old doctor had donned a Santa hat and carried a bag full of small boxes wrapped in brightly colored paper. Loretta sat primly next to him in his car as he drove. Under his breath he hummed Christmas carols and she couldn't help but smile at his cheer.

They arrived at the hospital, moving through its labyrinthine corridors, Dr. Bailey's appearance eliciting smiles from people as they went. Finally, they reached the ward where Dr. Bailey's patients were cared for. A grim looking nurse nodded at them but did not speak, and Loretta followed the doctor to the first door.

They visited three patients, people who Loretta knew by name and whose medical history she could recite practically by memory.

The doctor went through the same routine in each room: he'd come in smiling, laughing, greeting his patient. He'd sit by their bedside, talking with them, telling jokes, singing loudly and off key. The patients would laugh or smile as best they were able, then Dr. Bailey would present them with a small gift, shake their hand, and leave with a wink and a promise to see them soon.

The fourth and final patient they visited was George. He lay, pale and weak, against his pillows. A sheen of perspiration shone on his face, and his breathing was labored. Dr. Bailey entered this room more quietly than the others, almost reverentially. He sat next to George's bed and switched on the small lamp beside it.

Loretta gasped and stepped backward into the hall. As the light flicked on, a mass of shadows slid off George's bed and spread along the floor. Gray-black and viscous, Loretta lifted her foot from the tile as it inched toward her, afraid that if the shadows touched her, they'd slide their way up her legs like she had seen them do to George.

"Loretta!" Dr. Bailey's voice was a loud whisper. "Don't you want to come in and see George?"

She glanced up at the doctor, at the patient whose eyes were now open, yellowed and crusted with a thick discharge, looking at her through a haze of pain and medication. When she looked back down at the floor, there was no sign of the shadows, no sign of anything out of the ordinary.

With a shaking breath, she stepped forward into the room. She said hello to George and did her best to offer him a smile, then took a seat in the chair closest to the door, tucking her purse beneath her and folding her hands quietly in her lap.

Dr. Bailey's visit with George was far more subdued than the others. He spoke in low tones, leaned in close to hear George's feeble responses. There was no singing, only a murmured prayer and a clasping of hands before they departed, sneaking quietly out of the room as George drifted off into an uneasy sleep.

They made it all the way to the lobby before Loretta realized she'd left her purse behind.

"Run up and get it, my dear, and I'll pull the car around to the doors for you," Dr. Bailey said.

Loretta turned and faced the long walk back to the pulmonology ward. She yawned and rubbed her eyes as she made her way through the deserted hallways. She couldn't wait to get home, take off her shoes, eat some dinner, and spend time with her children.

The ward was quiet, the only sounds the quiet wheezing of the patients and the steady hum of the machines keeping some of them alive.

Loretta glanced into the first room as she passed it. One of their patients lay unmoving on the bed, deep in a medicated slumber. The second room was not a patient of Dr. Bailey's, but Loretta glanced in out of curiosity just the same. She stumbled back as her eyes took in the roiling shadows that filled the room, swirling around the bed while the patient shifted restlessly beneath the sheets.

Loretta glanced at the charge nurse and saw that she was watching her carefully, her eyes narrowed. Loretta forced a smile and walked on down the ward.

Two more rooms with nothing strange, and then the next...

Loretta stopped short. She could swear there was a person in the room, standing over the patient's bed. But visiting hours were long over. She took a step closer to the doorway, and the man — or the shadow in the shape of a man — dissolved in wisps of blackness which sank back down to the ground.

Behind her, the nurse cleared her throat quietly. Loretta turned to her, eyes wide with terror.

The nurse stared hard at her for a moment before she spoke. “You see it, too, don't you?” she asked.

Loretta's mind fumbled for an answer. “See... see what exactly?”

The nurse gave a sad smile. “The shadows. They come for them, you know, the shadows of their vice, they come near the end and claim what's theirs.”

Loretta's eyebrows furrowed in confusion. “The shadows of their vice? What do you mean?”

The nurse sighed, shuffled the papers in her hands, set them down on the desk in front of her.

"The *shadows,*" she said. "And don't shoot the messenger here, okay? I don't decide how it happens. But I've watched this ward long enough to know. Not everyone has them, you see, the shadows. Only the smokers — the heavy smokers. The three packs a day crowd. The shadows, as near as I can tell, they're... they're the manifestation of that vice, that addiction. And they come to claim the lives of those who succumbed to the addiction. They come to take what's theirs."

Loretta stared at the nurse in horrified silence for a moment, her brain trying to process what she'd just been told. It was unreal, impossible, wasn't it?

But she had seen the shadows, she *had.* A wave of goosebumps started on her neck and trickled down her arms. The nurse, seeing that Loretta didn't believe her, sighed and asked, "Do you need something? Why did you come back?"

Given a question she actually had an answer to, Loretta managed to speak again. "Oh, just... I left my purse behind, in George Harkin's room."

The nurse nodded and gestured toward the room, indicating that Loretta could go in and retrieve her bag.

The door was pulled to, and not wanting to disturb George's hard-won slumber, Loretta slipped around it as quietly as she could, trying not to let the light from the corridor beyond shine in George's face. She knelt and pulled her bag from beneath the chair she'd sat in fifteen minutes earlier. She tried her hardest not to look toward the bed, afraid of what she might see.

She had turned and was almost to the door again when she heard it: a low, guttural growl. She spun on the spot, eyes darting around the dark room.

George's eyes glowed dully in his face. He stared at her. His arm lifted weakly, dropped back to the bed. It lifted again, beckoning her forward.

She swallowed down a rising fear and stepped toward him. When she drew near enough, George's skeletal hand reached out and grasped her wrist.

His voice was a gravelly whisper as he spoke. “It's... killing me. It's... crushing me. Can't you see it?”

His eyes, wild, looked at something straight in front of him, and Loretta didn't dare glance in the same direction.

“It's... crushing me. Help... me.” George's eyes bulged as he tried to draw breath. His hand dropped from Loretta's wrist, and she took a few stumbling steps backward. Her hands flew to her mouth as she raised her eyes and saw the creature.

Perched atop George's chest, the shadowy imp became clearer and more defined as she watched. It was small, the size of the young chimpanzees she'd seen at the zoo with the kids last weekend, but its face was terrible, and pointed wings sprouted from its back. The thing had its long arms in front of it, its clawed hands pressed firmly against George's chest. It turned its head and grinned at her as it leaned forward, forcing more of its body weight on George's already weakened lungs.

George stared, unblinking, at the creature as it leered above him. His hands flapped feebly at his sides, a useless attempt to dislodge his own personal demon.

> Loretta could only watch in horror as George took one last, shuddering breath and went still, his head lolling to the side so that his wide and lifeless eyes pointed in her direction. The creature leaned back and surveyed its work, and then, in an instant, it melted into shadows which ran down the sides of the bed and returned to the places they had come from.
>
> Loretta clutched her purse to her chest and ran from the room. The nurse shot up from her chair at Loretta's frenzied approach.
>
> "What...?" she asked, but Loretta only shook her head in denial of what she'd just seen and kept going.
>
> The nurse's face took on a knowing look as she rushed around the desk and toward George's room.
>
> Loretta hurried, high heels clacking along the tiled floors as she ran, all the way through the hospital and out to where Dr. Bailey sat waiting in his car.
>
> She put in her resignation the next day. Soon afterward she got a job as a secretary in an insurance office, and she remained there until she retired in her sixties. She couldn't ever bring herself to go back to that hospital floor, and it was only when she was in her eighties and close to dying herself that she told my mother and I this story.

Chelsea finished her tale and looked around at her audience.

Half a dozen shocked faces stared back at her. For a moment, everyone was silent. Then Roger grinned and started laughing.

"I told you it was a good story!" He stood and started piling more wood onto the dwindling pile in the fire pit, stoking the flames up with one hand and lighting a new cigarette with the other.

The girl next to her, a girl Chelsea didn't know very well named Renee, looked at her curiously. "Is that really a true story?" she asked.

Across from them, Roger hooted his laughter. “Of course it's not really true. I mean, maybe old Granny Loretta thought it was true when she told it, but she'd gone a bit batty by then anyway, hadn't she, Chels?”

Chelsea gave a small shrug and Renee gave her a look both questioning and apologetic. When Chelsea didn't say anything else, Renee turned and began talking to the others around the campfire.

Chelsea sighed and shifted her legs, trying to get comfortable on the log which served as her seat.

She tried to let the dancing flames and the conversation around her lull her into a state of relaxation, but her eyes kept darting to the darkness around them, to the shadows that pulled forward from the forest beyond, the shadows that gathered like a cloak around Roger as he lit up his sixth cigarette of the night.

Burglar Man

He had watched the house for four days, and the woman for three.

That first day, he thought maybe the house was empty. After an entire afternoon of sitting and staring and not seeing a single soul go in or out the door or pass by a window, he had dared to sneak closer and peer inside.

Under the cover of twilight he had walked – slowly and calmly, so as not to attract attention – to the side of the house which sat in deepest shadow.

He glanced inside a window. The room was dim but even in the scant light he could see the gleam of expensive things: silver dishes and bronze statues and heavy crystal.

He felt a thrill of anticipation. This house was the mother lode. He could live off the profits of this job for months, years maybe. He could –

But then the light had switched on, a sign of life in the old place after all, and the burglar had ducked down low. He waited a moment before rising slowly back up, peeking in at the corner of the window.

At first he didn't see her. The room looked exactly the same as it had before, the soft yellow light now revealing even more treasures.

Then a slight movement caught his eye, and he stared in surprised amusement at the person who now sat in the expensive wingback chair just a few feet away from him.

She was old, but old didn't seem a strong enough word for it. Ancient, perhaps, would be a better choice. Her body was oddly proportioned, thick through the middle with scrawny arms and legs which seemed barely more than skin and bone.

A surprisingly thick shock of white hair was pulled back in a bun at the nape of her neck.

He could see one side of her face, so deeply wrinkled that it seemed covered in cracked shadows. She wore a white nightgown, its girlish lace and frills incongruent with her obvious age, and soft quilted slippers upon her feet.

Through a small chip in the corner of the window, he could just make out the sound of the woman humming, a tune which faded in and out and felt vaguely familiar. She held a book in her hands and seemed to be reading as she hummed.

The burglar laughed at his luck, then quickly clapped a hand over his mouth. He risked another peek at the old woman. She hadn't moved, hadn't reacted in the slightest to the noise outside her window. Not only was she ancient, but deaf or nearly so as well! His luck couldn't get any better.

He had stayed, that evening, crouched among the boxwoods below that window, until the light had winked out. He stood and stretched and then backed away to look once more up at the front of the house.

His eyes followed a chain of lights as the old woman made her way up to bed: First the octagonal window that he guessed would be over the stairs lit up for a few moments before going dark again, then a small window along the front – the bathroom, he presumed, and finally the lights of what must be the old woman's bedroom, which stayed lit for five minutes and then went out.

The entire house was dark; it would stay that way through all the long hours of the coming night.

The burglar wanted to get inside that house with a desire that made him jittery with excitement and impatience, but he knew better than to rush things. It would not do to barge in after just one day, assuming that the woman was alone.

There could be a son or a grandson coming along at any moment, home from some business trip or week-long visit with friends.

So, he waited and watched for three more long days. No one came to visit. The old lady never stepped foot outside. She must have moved about the house during the daytime, but with the sunlight glinting against the windows the burglar could not track her movement.

This did not worry him. He knew that each day, as the sun disappeared and the world grew dark, the light would switch on in that first room he had seen, some sort of library or office. Each evening, the old woman would sit in the wingback chair with a book, sometimes reading it, sometimes staring at the pages without turning them, for an hour.

And then each evening, the burglar followed the chain of lights as she progressed upstairs and into bed.

On the fourth night, he made his move. He had formulated the plan as he watched the house that day. While the old woman slept, he could empty the entire house – except for what was in her bedroom.

He knew that he would make out just fine with the rest of the house and that there was really no reason to push his luck by trying to get into that room. He knew it, but he was feeling lucky, and even more greedy than usual, so with a little thinking he worked it out in his mind. He would go through that entire house.

He knew just how to do it.

Sure enough, the sun set, the world went dark, and the light in the little library came on. The burglar took a quick peek through the window as he passed it, and the old biddy was right where she was supposed to be.

He crept on, along the side of the house and around the corner to the back, where the kitchen door would allow him access to the haul of his dreams.

The lock on the door was laughably old and he thought he'd make quick work of it. He glanced around at the dark yard beyond, checking for witnesses; this was an instinctual action but unnecessary in this situation: the property was private, with high hedges all around.

No one could have seen him even if they had been standing just the other side of the fence. He pulled out his tools and went to work on the lock, but after five frustrated minutes he had to admit that the old lock was more capable than he'd given it credit for. It wouldn't budge.

He looked around and chuckled. Just to the left of the door was a tall window with the top section open a couple of inches.

If the top part could go down, then the bottom part could go up.

He pressed his fingers hard against the glass and pushed upward. The window gave the slightest creak of resistance and then rose. It was no trouble at all then to simply duck and climb in, his feet coming to rest easily and silently on the old linoleum.

He was in the house.

Beyond the kitchen, the glow of the library light spilled out onto the hallway floor and puddled along the bottom step of a steep stairwell. It was possible, he knew, that he could creep right past the library door and up the stairs without being seen, especially if the old maid was as deaf as he thought she was.

But that was an unnecessary risk, if his guesses were correct. He knew that most of these old houses had a back stairway tucked away somewhere, a stairway once used by servants to move unobtrusively about the house.

He felt certain he would find one in this house.

He was right.

He found it behind a door which was made to look like just another cabinet along the kitchen wall: a set of wooden stairs which turned sharply several times before reaching the top floor.

The burglar stumbled up the uneven steps in the darkness, cursing under his breath as he went. The door at the top opened just as soundlessly as the kitchen door had, and he took a moment to consider the image of the old woman faithfully oiling every hinge in the old house.

The upstairs hallway was dark. Two doors stood closed on each side. The burglar paused for a moment, uncertain after the twisting stairs of which side of the hall faced the front of the house.

He tried one door, then another. Neither was the old woman's bedroom. He must have chosen the wrong side of the hall. He tried the doors on the opposite side. Neither of these were the right room, either.

He stood in the hall, scratching his chin in confusion. He thought over the layout of the house as he had imagined it while doing his planning. For a few minutes, he was stumped, and then the answer came to him: he had unknowingly bypassed the second floor while climbing stairs in the dark.

The space he now stood in was probably once the servants' quarters, tucked away in the cramped confines of the third floor.

Back to the stairs he went. Climbing down in the darkness, he proceeded with his arms out, fingertips trailing along the rough wooden walls, feet feeling cautiously ahead of him for each next step.

He stumbled once, scraping the back of his heel so hard along one step that he was certain he would have seen blood if he could see anything at all. He bit back a curse and forced himself to breathe slowly until his equilibrium righted itself.

After the first two sections of stairs, he stopped. He searched once more for a door and with relief his gloved hands wrapped around the protruding knob. The burglar took a deep breath, reminded himself of his plan, and cautiously pulled the door open.

The hallway was dark, but not pitch-black. All the doors on this floor were open, and just enough moonlight shone in through the windows to light his way.

He was confident now which side of the hall faced the front of the house, certain which doorway led to the old lady's bedroom, but he couldn't resist peeking into the other rooms along the way.

Every shelf and dresser was covered with expensive trinkets and tchotchkes.

The burglar smiled in the dark.

At the end of the hall, he entered the bedroom. Pale moonlight illuminated a room which looked more like a bridal chamber than an old woman's place of rest. Everything was white and lacy – the bedspread, the sheets, the canopy, the curtains.

White lace runners stretched across the top of a dresser and a vanity table.

It was to this last piece of furniture that the burglar's eyes were drawn. Spread across it were a hundred tiny treasures: a real silver hairbrush and mirror, a silver container of face powder, ivory and silver hair combs, crystal tumblers, rings and necklaces and brooches. An old-fashioned hat stand stood empty on one end, a Tiffany lamp on the other.

He reached out a hand toward the silver, then stopped. He had to be smart about this. If he took the things from the top of the vanity, she might notice. It would be safer to check the drawers; she would probably not open them and therefore not notice if something was missing.

He pulled open the first drawer, and in his head he let out a whoop of excitement. The drawer was divided into multiple sections and in each lay a ring, set with diamonds or rubies or sapphires or gems the burglar did not even know the name for but knew would fetch a high price.

He pulled a loot bag from inside his jacket and began filling it with the rings. In the next drawer he found another divider, these velvet-lined boxes filled with brooches of silver and gold and gems.

He was just dropping the last one into his bag when he heard it.

He paused, crouched over the vanity, one hand holding the bag, the other still inside it, and listened. His ears were met with the unmistakable sound of water running – very clear and very close.

The old woman was in the bathroom just next to the bedroom! The burglar tilted his wrist toward the window so that the moonlight shone on the cracked face of his watch.

It was far later than he'd thought – he cursed himself for wasting so much time up on the third floor – but the woman was ten minutes earlier than usual as well!

Why, tonight of all nights, would she come up early?

He closed the door gently, quietly, and then pulled tight the drawstring closure of his loot bag. He crept to the door and peeked around it. Bright light from the bathroom spilled out onto the floorboards of the hall.

The burglar began to panic, his heart pounding frantically in his chest. If he left the room he was in, he'd take the chance of being right in her line of sight. Even just rushing to the door directly across the hall was risky, and the longer he stood there considering his choices, the more chance there was that the old woman was on the verge of walking out of the bathroom.

In a flash the thought entered his mind that a little old lady was no match for him. He could knock her over and be out of the house before she managed to stand up again. But then he'd lose his chance, and all those expensive knick-knacks would stay on their shelves.

For half a second he considered that he could kill her and have the whole night ahead of him to ransack the place, but something in his conscience rejected that thought. He might be a criminal, a no-good burglar-man, but he was no killer.

In the room next door, the water shut off. He could hear the old lady humming to herself, the exact song she'd been humming four nights ago. He pictured her drying her hands and turning out the light and coming down the hall to the doorway where he himself now stood.

In a panic, and without really thinking, he took a few steps to the lace-covered bed, dropped to the ground, and scooted himself beneath the wooden frame.

Not a minute later, the bedroom light switched on, and the burglar watched from his hiding place as the old woman's slipper-covered feet shuffled into view.

He made himself breathe slowly, quietly. He told himself that his plan was not ruined, only altered a little. He reminded himself of the money he'd get from all the items he could steal in this house.

He convinced himself that he would just lay here quietly until he was sure the old lady was asleep and then carefully slide out from under the bed and go about his business in the rest of the house.

The woman came close to the bed and stopped for a moment. All he could see were the pink-flower-patterned slippers and the lacy hem of her nightgown. Then the woman stepped out of her slippers, leaving them with the toes just under the bed.

The burglar recoiled as much as he could from the woman's feet. They were gnarled and crooked, toes bent in painful-looking angles. The skin was dry and flaking, covered in age spots, the veins showing just beneath the surface like tiny purple roads across a grotesque landscape. Worst of all were the toenails–long, thick, brittle, yellow nails with jagged edges.

The burglar pressed his lips together tightly and held his breath, suppressing the urge to gag.

Finally, the old woman and her awful feet stepped away from the bed. The burglar turned his head to watch her as she hobbled toward the vanity.

The scrape of the vanity bench along the wooden floor sent vibrations through his stomach where it pressed against the boards. He could not see the woman herself, at least not above the ankles, but if he tilted his head just right he could watch her in the vanity mirror.

It was then that the burglar saw the most horrific chain of occurrences he had ever experienced in his life.

The woman leaned forward and looked at herself in the mirror, turning her face one way then another, running her fingers along her loose and drooping skin.

She licked her lips a few times and smiled at her own reflection. She reached her long, bony fingers inside her mouth and pulled out a set of dentures, dropping them into a crystal glass of water that sat on the vanity top.

This was unpleasant, but nothing the burglar hadn't seen before.

Then the woman leaned so close to the mirror that she almost touched it. With one hand she pulled down the lower lid of her left eye; with the other hand she slid a finger into the cavity beyond and popped out her eyeball.

The burglar gagged and swallowed back bile as she dropped the glass eye into another waiting crystal tumbler. The sagging flesh of her eyelid now drooped low, almost but not quite obscuring the pocket of pink-red flesh behind it.

Again, the woman turned her head from side to side, as if admiring herself, humming all the while.

She smacked her gummy mouth a few times and let out a girlish giggle that grated on the burglar's hearing like fingernails on a chalkboard.

A thought began to bloom inside his mind: this woman might be just a little bit crazy.

Still seated at the vanity, the woman picked up the silver-handled brush and made a few quick swipes at the sides of her head, smoothing back a few stray hairs.

Then, after carefully replacing the brush exactly where it had come from – *good thing I didn't take anything from the top, she would definitely have noticed it,* the burglar thought – she reached up with both arms, skin hanging loose and wobbling, and pulled the hair right off of her head.

A wig! She hung it carefully on one of the empty pegs of the hat rack. The burglar couldn't take his eyes off the awful sight that greeted him.

Her bare, hairless head was uneven, lumpy, covered in the same brownish spots and purpled veins that crisscrossed her feet.

An involuntary shudder passed through him, making the bed frame shift with a muffled thud.

Eyes wide, the burglar did his best to remain absolutely still. He held his breath and kept his eyes trained on the woman's reflection. She was hard of hearing, wasn't she?

Maybe she hadn't noticed the noise. Maybe she would turn out the light and get into bed soon and fall asleep quickly and this whole unanticipated nightmare would be over.

Maybe not.

"I know you're under there."

The woman's sing-song voice was high and unnerving, a child's voice in an ancient body. But how could she know he was there? Was she even talking to him? Was she talking to… a ghost, an imaginary friend?

The burglar remained still, hoping against hope that she was truly insane and simply talking to someone who was not there.

"Yes, you, man under my bed," she said, and the burglar gasped.

He watched in slow horror as the reflection of her one good eye turned and met his gaze in the mirror.

Of course! If he could see her then she could see him. How could he have been so stupid?

"I suggest you come out from there right this moment, young man," she said, and suddenly her voice was deeper, stern like some of his old teachers when they'd threatened him with a whipping.

"Now," she said, when he did not move.

Again the thought of knocking the woman over and running entered his mind. Again the thought of murdering her came and went.

All he knew for sure was that he must leave his hiding spot before he could do anything, so slowly he began to shift himself sideways.

He had managed to get under the bed with silence and skill. Getting out proved to be more difficult. His muscles were stiff from being forced into an uncomfortable position.

His left leg was asleep and sent tingling needles of pain up and down his body with every movement. His lungs felt half-crushed from barely breathing for the last ten minutes.

Slowly, with much thumping and scraping and cursing and more than a few splinters in his palms and belly, the burglar managed to get out from under the bed, and with one hand gripping the bedpost, he pulled himself to a standing position.

He raised his eyes to the old woman, deciding, finally, to simply make a run for it. Out the bedroom door, down the stairs, away from the house.

He hadn't managed the legendary plunder he'd hoped for, but he had enough jewelry stashed in the small loot bag inside his jacket to live on for a good while, and that would have to be enough.

The old maid, however, had other plans.

The third drawer of the vanity hung open, the one drawer he hadn't checked, and with a swift and smooth movement, the woman's gnarled hands grasped the revolver within and swung it upward.

She sat primly on her bench, an ancient hag to rival any old children's tale, gripping the gun with both hands and pointing it directly at the burglar's face.

He froze, the pins and needles along his left leg almost unbearable, still clinging to the bedpost, as he stared down the barrel of the gun.

For a moment they simply looked at each other, the old maid and the burglar man, he with his heartbeat pounding in his ears, and she humming cheerfully, that same tune he had heard before.

He realized that he did know the song: it was the music they played at weddings when the bride walked down the aisle.

Slowly, the woman stood. She kept the gun trained on him as she stepped closer. When she spoke, her voice was quiet, calm, a little breathy.

"We do find ourselves in quite a predicament here, don't we, young man? Whatever shall we do? I could call the police, but I really see no need to do that, do you? No, I have a much better idea. You, sir, are here to rob me. To spirit away all my jewels and family heirlooms, to take that which is mine and to sell it for money to fund your nefarious ways, is that correct?"

The burglar nodded, and the old woman went on.

"I have no intention of letting you run away with my prized possessions. But…"

Her tongue darted out, a pale monstrous appendage, and licked her thin and bloodless lips.

"I think it's possible we may come to a sort of agreement. A partnership, if you will. Interested?"

The man felt both confused and intrigued. This old lady had managed to shock him, to take him completely by surprise. He gave a slight nod in answer to her question.

"Alright, young man. Here is my proposal: you wish to live in luxury. I have the luxury you desire. I will gladly share it with you. But I demand something from you in return. You see, my dear, I am but an old maid. I have never known the touch of a man's hands upon my body, never been married, never been loved."

She took two more steps toward him, so that the gun pushed gently against his belly. With one hand she reached up and stroked his cheek, and the man recoiled.

Faster than should have been possible at her age, the hand which had just touched him so lovingly pulled back and slapped him across the face, and with the other hand she shoved the gun harder against his gut.

"Listen, young man. This is your final and only choice. You will marry me, live here with me, take care of me, make love to me here in the bed where I have dreamed so long of a lover's touch. You will do all of these things for the rest of my days, or I will shoot you right now, bang!"

She backed away a step, raised the gun to point directly between his eyes.

"What will it be, sir? Don't try to run, I'm a crack shot and you'll not stand a chance. Don't think you can weasel out of it, because if you agree and don't fulfill your end of the bargain, there will be hell to pay. Choose now. Young man, you're going to marry me, or I'll blow off the top of your head."

The burglar looked at the old woman in front of him. He looked at her bulging middle, her stick-thin legs and the loose skin of her arms. He looked at her teeth and her big glass eye floating in the crystal tumblers atop the vanity. His eyes roamed quickly over the mottled skin of her scalp, her gummy smile, the gaping hole where her eye should be.

She blocked the doorway, and somehow he knew that he'd never get past her, that at this range even this ancient woman could easily shoot him.

He considered what it would feel like to have her saggy, naked body pressed against him, and bile rose in his throat once more.

Seeing no escape, he raised his hands in surrender and spoke the last six words of his wretched life.

"Lady, for the Lord's sake, shoot."

A look of furious anger came over the woman's face. The shot rang out, thunderously loud. The bed, once the snow-white of a bridal dream, turned slowly crimson as the man's blood soaked the sheets and blankets.

Carlton County Gazette

May 25, 1946

BURGLAR GETS WHAT'S COMING TO HIM - Last night, long-time Carlton County resident, descendant of our town founder, beloved spinster Miss Martha June Carlton fought off and shot an intruder in her home.

The thief gained access through a back window and laid in wait for Miss Carlton in her bedroom after taking most of her jewelry.

According to statements by Miss Carlton, who was visibly shaken, the man attempted to molest her in the most unbecoming fashion but was surprised when Miss Carlton pulled her grandfather's gun from a nearby drawer and defended her own life and honor by shooting the dastardly crook square between the eyes.

Groups of concerned citizens have already been hard at work at the old Carlton Mansion this morning, cleaning up the mess.

HUNGRY

The wagon had once been a bright emerald green. Faded gold lettering arced across the back, the paint peeling and fluttering away in the late autumn wind.

Trout & Son's
Traveling Circus

One end of the wagon sat against an ancient tree trunk; at the other end, the wagon tongue was braced against a great gray boulder. Drifts of dry leaves gathered around the old wheels.

The forest was quiet. The great beast slept fitfully in its cage.

Gilbert Trout – the *Son* of Trout & Son – had tried his best. He had grown up in the circus caravan, learning a little of this skill, a bit of that trick, the basics of how to care for the animals.

His main purpose, however, the reason for which he had been born, was to learn to run the circus as a whole, to one day take over for his father and keep the caravan rolling from town to town, entertaining the masses.

Eventually the time had come for the younger Trout to step into his father's shoes – worn, patched shoes though they were. For a few years, it seemed the son would eclipse the father in his business acumen.

The circus grew; entertainers flocked to the ringmaster's wagon, begging to join the great Trout & Son as they traveled across the country. New tents, higher and wider, were sewn in strips of green and white.

New signs were painted, gaudy and glaring and sure to attract the attention of every small boy in a hundred-mile radius. The circus menagerie grew; new wagons were built, set in with strong steel bars, to keep the more dangerous denizens safely contained.

Gilbert, riding high on the success of his business ventures, courted and married Louisa Pye, daughter of the infamous Strong Man. Within three years, Louisa had pushed out a couple of fat, healthy babies.

The circus was successful. The family was growing. The Trout name would carry on.

Old Grandpa Trout felt a satisfaction he would never have dreamed possible all those years ago when he first set out to find his own place in the world.

He was happy to ride along in his little wagon at the end of the caravan with Grandma Trout, his wife of forty years, swaying on the seat beside him.

But as so often happens, the good was *too* good to last. Hard times fell on the country. At first, the circus was a welcome distraction to the people caught in a downward spiral of poverty and despair, a few hours of mindless entertainment worth the price of admission.

However, the time came – and it came quickly – that even the few cents required to enter the striped tent became too much to ask. The shows drew progressively smaller crowds; the small savings Gilbert Trout had hidden away were fast depleted.

It was a sad day when the caravan broke apart. A hundred wagons rolled away in all directions, performers and workers heading off in groups, in pairs, or alone to find whatever scraps of life they could scavenge in the surrounding towns.

The great Trout & Son's zoo was divided and sent away. The smaller animals went easily enough with their trainers. The bright striped tigers found homes in a zoo along the road. The trained horses were sold for a pittance to desperate farmers, trading in their days as high-stepping entertainers for hours spent in cheerless toil.

Finally, all that remained of the traveling circus set off along a dusty road, headed north. Gilbert Trout's wagon, with Louisa at the reins and young George and Lolly bouncing along in the back, took the lead.

Grandpa and Grandma Trout brought up the rear, their own wagon loaded down with as many provisions as the family could gather.

In between, Gilbert himself drove the wagon that held the two animals which remained. Perched on Gilbert's shoulder, his tail wrapped around the man's neck, sat Coco the monkey, a look of resigned determination in his small, intelligent eyes.

Within the wagon, behind the strongest steel bars that man could fashion, hidden from view by great swaths of heavy canvas tied down with thick rope, Kodiak, the great man-eater, growled and paced tight circles in his cramped prison.

Gilbert Trout listened to the steady rumble of the beast's grumbling as the wagons rolled on toward an unknown future.

The cabin was fortuitous.

The Trout family – Grandma, Grandpa, Papa Gilbert, Mama Louisa, young George and Lolly, and of course Coco the monkey – traveled for weeks before they found it.

Food had grown scarce; even well-laid provisions don't stretch far when six people, a primate, and an enormous bear need feeding every day. Besides that, the family was unhappy.

The adults were falling rapidly into deep depression; the children were bored and restless.

The path into the woods was barely discernible; were it not for little George's eagle eyes, they might not have noticed it at all. After a brief deliberation between both Trout and Son, the wagons were turned off the main trail and onto the soft dirt path into the shadowy forest.

Half a day's ride brought them to the cabin. Though clearly deserted, the building seemed sound enough, and with colder weather on the way, Gilbert Trout knew he needed a shelter – more sturdy and secure than an old, rocking wagon – in which to keep his family safe for the coming winter.

Being both ingenious and industrious, it wasn't long at all before the Trout's had settled in to a more or less comfortable existence.

The space was small, it was true, for four adults, two children, and a monkey, but for people used to making do with a home the width and breadth of a wagon bed, it was luxurious enough.

The wagons themselves were disassembled, the wooden boards repurposed as table and chairs and bed frames. Mama and Grandma Trout ripped apart the old green-and-white striped tent canvases, sewed them into bags, stuffed them with fallen leaves and great tufts of dried grass, and turned them into mattresses and pillows.

Papa and Grandpa Trout slowly learned to hunt the deer that lived in the forest. Little George, after much trial and error, perfected his own design for a trap which caught them rabbit and squirrel.

Mama and Lolly filled buckets with the berries which grew in abundance in the woodland gullies.

Before the first snows fell, Mama and Papa Trout set out for the nearest town. They left the cabin that morning riding two horses; they returned after dark with none, trudging slowly up the path, Gilbert pulling a small cart loaded with packages.

They had made good trades. If they were smart and careful, they would have enough food to last six people and one monkey through the winter.

But Kodiak, the beast, the great brown bear from the north, grew hungry.

Papa Trout stood just outside the small cabin where his family had taken up residence. He breathed in great lungful's of crisp morning air and watched as the sun's meager light slowly spread across the forest floor.

Behind him, the house was filled the hustle and bustle of the day's beginnings.

It was a beautiful morning, and his family was secure for the time being. Gilbert Trout should have been content, satisfied, thankful, and he was, but one thing, one problem, paced and grumbled through his otherwise happy thoughts.

The bear.

There'd been no way to get rid of it; no zoo wanted it, and they couldn't just turn it loose. Gilbert had paid a handsome sum for the bear three years prior, awed by its massive size and ferocious snarl.

The hunters from whom he purchased the animal seemed glad to be rid of it; they called it a man-eater, and in the half-whispers they shared amongst themselves, Gilbert heard mysterious things.

Not only a man-eater, they said in hushed tones, but half-man itself.

The bear, they said, could stand and walk on two legs like a man, and they swore that at times, deep within the night, the beast's rumbling growls took on the shape of words and the bear *spoke*.

Of course, Gilbert had laughed at this preposterous idea, but he'd bought the bear and used the story to attract gullible customers just the same.

He'd seen the bear walk on two legs like a man only once; since that time the creature had been confined to its wagon-cage, unable to stretch to its full height. They fed the beast with hunks of meat skewered on long sticks which they poked between the bars.

The hay which acted as both bed and bathroom was mucked out in much the same way: with long-handled brooms that allowed the work to be done from a safe distance.

He'd never heard the bear talk.

Until now.

While his parents, his wife, and his children went about their morning chores in the house behind him, Gilbert Trout stood, staring at the bear. He had slipped out the door while it was still dark, desperate for a few quiet moments to himself before the day began.

The last pale streaks of moonlight had glimmered across the faded gold paint, highlighting the bear's cage some fifty yards or so from the cabin. Gilbert stepped slowly, quietly, toward the wagon.

The wind picked up, rushing through the treetops with a sibilant roar; leaves scurried across the ground and swirled into the air, whipping against Gilbert's face and arms as he walked.

Just as quickly as it had started, the wind died, cut off as sharply as secret whisperings when the subject of conversation walks into the room.

In that sudden and unexpected silence, he heard it.

A steady rumble came from within the cage, and within that rumble were *words*.

Hungry. Hungry. Hungry. I'll eat you. I'll eat you. I'll eat you, too.

Gilbert backed away, shaking his head, a wild bubble of laughter rising up and choking him as he swallowed it back. It was impossible. It couldn't be.

Could it?

Gilbert did not raise the canvas covers from the wagon cage that morning as he did most days. He did not spear chunks of deer meat to push through the bars at the huge brown beast within.

He did not muck the cage.

He did not do these things for a whole week.

He left the bear alone. Left it to sit in its own filth. Left it to starve.

The bear bore this abandonment in near-silence. But each morning, when Gilbert went out to break the ice from the top of the water barrel, filled with bucketful's from the nearby stream, each morning as he passed by that old green wagon, he heard the growling speech.

Hungry. Hungry. Hungry.

The first heavy snow fell early in December. Grandpa and Papa Trout were caught out in it, hunting, and though they returned home before supper, their appearance met with cries of relief, the world had already fallen into a disquieting darkness. Gilbert shivered in the cold, as he paused at cabin door.

He turned his head and looked out into the darkness of the night. Moonlight reflected back from the glistening snow, making the shadow of the bear's cage stand out in sharp relief.

Above the howling of the wind, above the cacophony of happy voices waiting for him inside, he heard three distinct and troublesome sounds.

The scrape of sharp claws along a worn wooden floor as the bear paced.

The creak of old, brittle wood as an animal a thousand pounds strong pressed against the sides of its prison.

And the voice, the low rumble of inhuman words.

Hungry. I'll eat you. Hungry. I'll eat you.

Hungry.

Hungry.

Hungry.

Gilbert shivered again; this time it had nothing to do with the cold. He closed the door firmly against the snow, the darkness, and the beast.

Supper was a happy affair, at least for those without bothersome thoughts meandering slowly though their minds. Gilbert found himself nodding off at the table, exhausted from so many weeks of hard labor.

Grandma Trout put a hand to his forehead and exclaimed that he was feverish. Despite his feeble protestations, Papa Trout was put to bed early.

The room drifted in and out of focus. Voices swelled and diminished. The heat from the stone fireplace seemed to wash over him in waves, and Gilbert drifted into a deep sleep.

A sleep so deep that he did not hear when his wife called for more water to be brought in. He did not hear his young son volunteer to walk the short distance to the water barrel and fetch in a bucketful.

He did not hear him open the door and disappear into the night.

Young George Trout pulled the cabin door shut behind him. He was old enough now to help out, and with Papa sick in bed, he guessed that made him the man of the house.

He puffed out his chest and took a couple of swaggering steps toward the small lean-to where the water barrel and several sealed casks of dried goods were stored.

He stopped. He scratched his head, puzzled. Something was not right. Something was out of place though it took a moment for George to figure out just what it was.

The snow around the lean-to was melted away in a wash of water. Scattered further across the ground were a thousand tiny shapes that George, upon closer inspection, recognized as dried beans.

These things were curious.

The next revelation was terrifying.

Bear tracks. Enormous ones.

George stood, frozen, as his eyes lifted to the old wagon wedged between a tree trunk and a boulder. The canvas covering flapped in the wind, attached only barely at one upper corner. The steel bars still stood straight and strong, but beyond them…

Beyond them, George could see the moonlit forest.

The back of the wagon was gone.

Green-painted boards with gilded gold lettering lay in splintered disarray across the snowy ground.

Behind him, a presence. A rank smell, wild and feral. A heat that radiated against his skin, a blazing breath on the back of his neck. A guttural, rumbling growl, with words hidden just beneath it.

Hungry. So hungry. I ate a barrel of beans. I drank a barrel of water. I'll eat you too.

Then young George Trout knew only a hot, wet darkness, and nothing more.

"What is taking that boy so long?" Mama Trout tutted from inside the warm cabin. "Lolly, go out and tell your brother to hurry along."

The girl did not even have time to notice the tracks before the voice rumbled low in her ear.

Hungry. So hungry. I ate a barrel of beans. I drank a barrel of water. I ate a little boy, and I'll eat you, too.

With the tiniest of shrieks, Lolly Trout joined her brother in the great bear's stomach.

Grandma Trout was next.

Growl. Gulp. Gone.

Grandpa Trout came after.

Growl. Gulp. Gone.

Mama Trout came out, irritated to no end with her family's shenanigans.

Growl.

Gulp.

Gone.

Papa Trout woke to small paws against his face. Coco sat on his chest, gibbering excitedly. Gilbert looked around; the cabin was empty, though the fire still blazed merrily. He sat up in bed, rubbed his eyes, and stretched.

Coco jumped from the bed to the nearby table, chattering constantly. Gilbert thought he must be dreaming still, or his fever was higher than he thought, because he almost heard words in the monkey's wild sounds. He shook his head, called out for his wife, his children, his parents, anyone.

No one answered.

Gilbert rose slowly from the bed. The room spun for a moment, then righted itself. He walked to the door, opened it, and peered out. The cold air washed over his heated skin, a blessed relief. Outside all was calm and quiet.

Gilbert stepped out. Snow melted beneath his footsteps, soaking through his socks. He paused, listening, eyes narrowed as he looked from one skeletal tree to the next. Where were they? Where had his family gone? Was he even really awake, or was this all just a dream?

The snarl behind him told him this was, whether waking or sleeping, assuredly a nightmare.

Gilbert turned slowly. The great beast from the north's muzzle jutted forward, thick ropes of saliva dripping to hiss against the snow-covered ground.

Dark and horrifyingly intelligent eyes stared directly into Gilbert's own.

Hungry, it said. *So hungry.*

Gilbert gulped; the spittle stuck in his throat and he choked, bringing tears to his eyes. "Where are they? What have you done with them? Where is my family?"

The bear shuffled closer; Gilbert could not help but notice that the beast's belly had swollen to an unfathomable size. He swore, for the briefest moment, that he could see movement within that diabolical stomach, swore that he saw the shape of a hand pressing outward.

Gilbert lifted his eyes once again to meet the bear's glare.

Hungry.

The sound rumbled from the bear's throat and echoed around the small clearing.

So hungry. Still so hungry. I ate barrel of beans. I drank a barrel of water. I ate a little boy. I ate a little girl. I ate an old woman. I ate an old man. I ate a young woman, and I'll eat you, too!

Gilbert Trout, being the largest member of the family, took a little longer to slither down the giant bear's gullet, but in short time he joined his family in the cramped and malodorous confines of the bear's stomach.

Coco peeked around the edge of the still-open door. He remained uncharacteristically quiet for a few moments, contemplating his next move.

He watched as the impossibly huge bear lumbered slowly across the clearing. Coco could just hear the sobs of the people trapped within the beast's gut.

The monkey looked around at the dark and dangerous forest. His eyes darted from tree to tree, branch to branch.

He made up his mind. He knew what he had to do.

The bear turned as quickly as he was able at the sudden chattering which filled the air. He raised his upper lip in a snarl at the sight of the damned monkey, dancing around the clearing.

He was full, so full now, and the people inside his belly would not seem to settle down and accept their fate. He should just leave the monkey be, let it scramble off the fend for itself in the woods beyond.

But no. One last little treat, and then he would find a place to settle in and sleep through the winter.

The bear charged.

The monkey ran, jumped, scampered up the nearest tree. He hopped from branch to branch, chattering his taunts down to the ponderous beast below.

The bear let out a roar, the sound echoing through the trees, and within the roar the monkey heard the words.

I ate barrel of beans. I drank a barrel of water. I ate a little boy. I ate a little girl. I ate an old woman. I ate an old man. I ate a young woman. I ate a young man, and I'll eat you, too!

The monkey threw down his own words, a rapid-fire babble, a challenge.

Catch me if you can, then!

The monkey leaped from tree to tree, laughing all the while, until finally he came to a rest, panting, in the highest tree he could find.

The bear seemed to chuckle, a low, rolling sound like tumbling gravel. He stood to his full height, his hind legs barely supporting the weight of his roiling belly.

First one massive paw wrapped around the tree trunk, then the other. Sharp claws dug in as the bear climbed, quick and quiet, up to the branch where the monkey perched.

Coco glanced over his shoulder at the approaching beast. He would have to time things just right, he would have to wait until the last possible moment.

The bear reached the branch. Slowly he began to inch his way along its narrow girth.

Coco turned and watched as the giant crept nearer. The monkey backed away, slowly, little by little, toward the narrowest end of the precarious perch.

It happened suddenly.

The crack as the limb snapped reverberated through the forest and was heard in the town ten miles away.

Coco jumped clear at the last moment, leaping with ease onto the next tree over.

The bear, clinging for life to the falling branch, let out a pitiful roaring wail as he fell to the ground, thirty feet below.

The snow turned red with the bear's blood as its swollen belly burst open. Covered in filth and vile things they did not wish to examine too closely, each member of the Trout family stood, wiped the muck from their faces, and stumbled away from the furry carcass.

Gilbert Trout, still half-convinced he was mired in a fevered dream, held his children against his chest and laughed.

"Ha ha!" he crowed. "Ha ha! I'm out!"

His family joined him in laughter.

"I'm out!" the children cried.

"I'm out!" both of the grandparents shouted.

"I'm out?" Mama trout whispered, running her hands along her body to make sure she was still all in one piece.

Above them, Coco the monkey screeched his own laughter. He scrambled down the tree and joined the family on the ground.

And Gilbert Trout could swear that among the monkey's high-pitched babble, he heard the words *Ha ha! I'm out, 'cause I never was in!*

The Trout family discovered that winter that bear meat was immensely filling, if a little gamey.

When spring arrived, the whole family was happy and healthy. The womenfolk found that they were quite adept at gardening, and the menfolk grew better at hunting.

In time the Trout's would make regular trades with the nearby townsfolk for those things they could not grow or produce for themselves.

All in all, they created a nice little life, there at the cabin in the woods. Coco the monkey was loved, pampered, and spoiled rotten by all the members of the Trout family for the rest of his days.

Over time, the remnants of the old green wagon rotted away into nothingness, and when young Lolly Trout married the son of the town banker, she took with her as part of her dowry a bearskin rug more enormous than any the townspeople had ever seen.

Cries From the Attic

2020

"You sure about this?" Brandon asks, looking up the wide front stairs of the old mansion.

"Why?" Jessica, his girlfriend, pokes him playfully in the ribs. "You scared?"

Brandon scoffs dramatically and turns to their cameraman, Eddie.

"Let's roll then," he says, and Eddie nods, raising his camera to his shoulder and pointing it at Jessica.

She makes her way to the top step and sits down. "This good for the background segment?"

Brandon backs up a few steps and holds his hands up as if framing the shot. "Yeah, yeah, this is good."

Eddie adjusts a few things on the camera, then kneels on one knee and gives Jessica a silent thumbs-up.

"Hello, all our spooky, kooky friends out there!" Here Jessica flashes a smile and gives a little wave. "Tonight we're investigating this gorgeous old wreck, the Sherman house. Now, the Sherman house is known for one kind of haunting and one kind only, but that one extra special thing has been enough to scare off various owners and tenants for close to a century. And this one is a good one, friends. Because this one has – well, don't let me get ahead of myself here.

"The story goes like this: one day, the man of the house, one James Sebastian Sherman, who, judging by the research I've done, was a real

A-hole, if you know what I mean, one day he goes completely crazy, murders his wife and newborn baby up in the attic, then slashes his own wrists before the cops can bust in and stop him. He's half-dead already when the police break in, and he's mumbling the same words over and over…"

1940

The marriage was a mistake. Victoria Sherman had known it from that first day, that first night, those first few hours when at last they were left to themselves without guardians or chaperones. She had seen him then, finally, for what he really was, and she had known in her heart that she would never be happy again.

James Sebastian Sherman was a monster.

Not a monster in the way most people would think, not a vampire or a werewolf or even a ghoul. No, James Sebastian Sherman was nothing but a man with cruelty in his heart and violence in his veins.

Victoria learned to stifle her screams when he dragged her to the bedroom each night. She learned to hide the bruises and the cuts with long sleeves and high-necked dresses and regular applications of pan-cake make-up. She watched carefully for all the little signs that meant James's temper was close to flaring, and she learned all the ways in which she must be quiet, obedient, subservient.

Then came the day when Victoria realized that her monthly flow had not come as it should have. She counted days in her head, frantic, and concluded that she was two weeks late. A panic consumed her; a fear greater than she had ever known pulsed through her with each unsteady thump of her heart.

James took the news surprisingly – suspiciously – well. Victoria instructed Cook to make his favorite dinner. She put on the dress he had picked out for her, arranged her hair just the way he liked it. She asked him questions about himself as they ate, so that he could ramble on about his favorite subject.

She told him over dessert.

"James, darling, I have something to tell you. I – we – well, we're expecting a little someone. Sometime in December, I would think."

James stared at her, rolling the last bite of his cheesecake around in his mouth a few times before he spoke.

"Is it mine?"

Victoria held back the anger that welled inside her at the question. How could it be anyone else's? She was never allowed to leave the house unless she was on James's arm and was allowed no visitors. But to show her anger and her hurt would only set him off, so she knelt beside his chair, placed a hand softly on his arm, and gazed up at him with what she hoped appeared to be a look of love as she said softly, "Of course it is, darling. There's no one but you."

James wiped his face with his napkin and nodded his head once. "Very good then."

And that was that.

For the next seven months, Victoria lived a life more peaceful than she'd thought would ever be possible again. Her condition seemed to switch off her husband's desire for her body, and though she knew that he spent many of his nighttime hours downtown in the houses of ill repute, she could not bring herself to be bothered by it.

Let the other women have him, forever, for all she cared.

In the daytime, too, James seemed gentler. Oh, he was not cured completely, Victoria was not naive enough to believe that. She sensed the anger and the arrogance and the violence simmering just beneath the surface.

But James seemed to pull it back, to hold it in, and though he still occasionally spoke sharply to her, for those seven glorious months he did not lay a hand on her in any way.

As the time for the baby's birth drew near, Victoria began to feel a nagging worry. As the child within her developed and kicked and rolled, her maternal instinct grew sharp and strong.

Victoria tried not to let her mind play out the many awful scenarios that might occur should this child incur its father's wrath, but the scenes snuck into her dreams, turning them to nightmares.

Victoria began making plans. She waited until James was in a good mood and brought up the idea of the nursery. She told him she thought the large attic space would be ideal, with all the sunlight that filtered in from its many windows.

What she really meant was that the attic would be best because it would keep the child as far away as possible from its father, where cries in the night would not reach his ears and messy toys could not block his path and infuriate him.

James gave his disinterested approval.

Victoria created a nursery. Her maid, Cecily, and the housekeeper, Mrs. Dodson, were happy to help, though the smiles they bestowed upon the expectant mother were laced with sadness.

The walls were painted a cheerful yellow, the color of butter or spring sunrises. A crib was brought in, and a small dresser. A rocking chair sat on a pale green rug just beside a window that overlooked the street below. White lace curtains fluttered in the autumn breeze.

A bed was placed in the corner of the room, for Victoria herself.

When the time came, when Victoria felt those awful crushing pains inside her, no doctor was called. James wouldn't hear of it; no strangers were allowed in the house.

But Mrs. Dodson had six children and fourteen grandchildren of her own, and Cecily was the oldest of eleven, and between them they brought Victoria safely through the haze of pain and blood.

Mrs. Dodson placed the baby in Victoria's tired arms and proclaimed it a girl.

James Sebastian Sherman was not at home. He had left early that morning for meetings in town and stopped off that evening at the Red House.

By the time he came home, stumbling drunk and smelling of other women, Victoria and the baby were safely tucked away in the attic.

When he finally dragged himself from bed the next morning and made his way up to the attic nursery, he had but one question: "What is it? Boy or girl?"

Victoria, in a clean nightgown and robe, sat in the chair near the window, the swaddled child held lovingly against her. "It's a girl, darling. I – I haven't named her yet, I thought perhaps you'd like to –"

James made an ugly noise in his throat. "A girl? Ugh. What do I care about a girl?"

Victoria watched in angry silence as her husband turned and walked out of the room. Tears streamed down her face and fell onto the blankets that wrapped her child.

She named the girl Amanda, for the name meant "worthy of love," and she intended, despite her husband's obvious feelings toward the child, to make sure that her daughter knew that she was, in fact, worthy.

Days and nights passed, the sun rising and falling, darkness filling most of the hours as autumn changed over into winter. James was away more often than he was home, gone sometimes for days at a time.

Victoria did not miss him.

Ensconced in the attic nursery, where she slept in the corner bed and had Cook send up all her meals so that she needn't be away from her child for even the briefest of moments, she accepted that her sole mission now in life was to provide safety and happiness for her daughter.

On the fifth of January, the storm hit.

Pale blue skies changed suddenly to gray, and then the world went white as the blizzard swept in. James paced irritably in his study as Victoria rocked baby Amanda calmly up in the attic.

A twilight gloom descended over the house though it was barely past noon. Servants scurried about, building up fires and lighting extra lamps against the darkness.

Victoria moved the rocking chair closer to the small attic fireplace and continued rocking.

James went on pacing. He ran his hands through his hair again and again, frustration and annoyance building. He had intended to take a carriage downtown and then to walk secretly to the backdoor district where the Red House stood, full of rooms in which sultry women waited hungrily for men like him.

But there were no carriages to be had today.

The world seemed to be empty of people beyond those in his house. His lust strained painfully against his trouser-front and he muttered curses under his breath as he walked.

Then, all at once, the realization hit him: he had a wife.

Though not nearly as experienced in providing pleasure as the women of the Red House, she would do in a pinch.

He set off up the stairs.

Victoria was drowsing in front of the fire when the door slammed open. Amanda startled momentarily in her mother's arms at the sound then settled back to sleep.

The door closed again, and the lock engaged with an ominous click. Victoria looked up, half-asleep and confused, as James strode quickly toward her. It took her only a second, however, to recognize the look in his eyes as he stood leering over her.

"James, I – the baby –" she stammered.

"Put the baby down," he growled.

With trembling legs, Victoria stood. She walked to the crib, bouncing and shushing the baby as she went. She laid Amanda down and patted her gently until she quieted.

She turned to face her husband.

He was on her in an instant, like an animal, snarling and ripping at her clothing, hands rough on her arms as he shoved her to the floor and mounted her there on the pale green rug.

He pushed inside her, inside her flesh still tender from the birth, and Victoria let out a high shriek at the unexpected pain. James clamped a hand over her mouth.

Too late. In her crib, the baby began to cry.

Victoria felt herself overcome with a strength she had not known she possessed. She fought against her husband, kicking and biting, writhing beneath him.

He slapped her once, twice, hard. She screamed and cursed at him, arms flailing. He caught her hands, pinned her down, spat in her face.

The baby wailed, louder and louder.

James's hands dropped to Victoria's throat, squeezing hard as if to silence both her shrieks and the child's at once.

A darkness seemed to invade the room, a darkness which had nothing to do with the storm outside, but which seemed to rise instead like a black mist from James himself.

Victoria thought for an instant that his eyes flashed red as he pressed against her windpipe. The whole room seemed to spin, Amanda's cries caught in a whirlpool, visible streams of audible sound that spiraled around them.

Victoria's strength faded, her arms dropped to her sides, her voice no more than a cry in her own mind. Deprived of oxygen, her brain sent frantic messages to muscles that could no longer respond.

Minutes passed.

James, both enraged and aroused by the fight, dropped his hands to the floor and pumped his seed into his wife's still-warm corpse. He rolled over, off her unmoving body, and the world went black around him.

Minutes later, James woke with a start. Quiet whimpers came from the nearby crib. He looked at Victoria, her lifeless eyes gazing toward the child, one arm outstretched in the same direction.

James stood. He walked slowly to the crib. He rested his arms on the top rail and stared down at his daughter with cold hatred in his eyes.

He leaned over the rail as far as he could, and his hot breath hit the baby in the face as he hissed.

"See what you made me do? See what you made me do! If you'd just shut up for one minute, it would have all been alright. It's your fault. It's your incessant wailing that made it happen!" He poked at the child, hard, with his finger, and her cries crescendoed once more.

He plucked a pillow from the floor and held it suspended over the baby's reddened face. For a moment he stood, staring down at the child, his child, then a hellish grin spread across his lips, and he lowered the pillow.

There was banging at the door, the loud pounding of multiple fists. He heard the tremulous cries of Mrs. Dodson, the quiet weeping of Cecily, and another voice, a man's voice, deep and authoritative, demanding that he open the door this instant.

James recognized, in some still-lucid section of his mind, that the man was a policeman.

He looked at his wife's body on the floor, at the small unmoving bundle in the crib. He began to laugh, wild, maniacal, diabolical laughter that echoed against the high rafters.

James looked around, eyes wide and glassy, until he spotted Victoria's sewing scissors on the table near her bed.

He snatched up the scissors and opened them until they formed one long, sharp weapon. He did not feel it as the blade cut into his wrists, over and over again.

He watched in fascination as the blood welled up, slowly at first, then pumping ferociously over his arms.

He stumbled against the rocking chair and sat down hard. The scissors dropped to the floor with a dull thud. Crimson pooled around him as the pounding and shouting at the door continued.

The policemen who finally forced open the door were faced with a scene that would haunt their minds for the rest of their days.

Victoria, defiled and dead upon the floor.

James, still laughing weakly as his head lolled against his shoulder, his arms held out in front of him, his life draining slowly away.

And the most awful sight of all, when they finally checked the crib.

"What's he saying?" asked the officer in charge.

James's mouth moved incessantly, though only the faintest of whispers came out. One of the younger officers approached him slowly, cautiously.

James made no move to stop the officer as he leaned down close in order to catch the words.

The officer stood back up, his face pale.

"Well?" demanded his captain.

The officer gulped.

"He's saying, 'You'll never take me. I'll never leave.'"

2020

"...he's mumbling the same words over and over: 'I'll never leave.'"

Jessica gives an overdramatic shiver and looks into the camera with wide eyes before continuing.

"We've dug up information on six of the people who have owned the house since then, and all have reported similar occurrences: on cold winter nights, a baby's cry can be heard echoing through the house. When people try to locate the source of the sound, they're always led to the attic. Bum-bum-bum!" Jessica laughs.

"But this is where it gets interesting, folks. Because once people go into the attic, they're attacked! Some people report the feeling of ghostly hands closing around their necks, some the feeling of long scratches along their forearms. There are even…"

– here she leans in toward the camera –

"two instances, back in the 1950s, of people going up to that attic and disappearing, never to be seen again! Now, friends, we, your Ghostly Threesome, are going to go inside this very house and see exactly how much truth there is to these rumors."

Jessica holds her expression for a moment, until Eddie gives her another thumbs-up and lowers the camera.

"That was great, babe," Brandon says, kissing Jessica on the top of her head. The three gather at the front door as Brandon unlocks it with the keys he's been given by the realty office.

With the door closed behind them, they stand for a few moments letting their eyes adjust to the darkness.

"OK, phones up, people," Brandon orders, and they all lift their phones, turning on their cameras.

"Eddie, you do a preliminary sweep of the first floor. I'll take the second. Babe," he turns to Jessica, "you get the attic."

She wiggles her eyebrows at him like he's just suggested a kinky sex game and turns to ascend the old staircase, giggling as she goes.

Eddie rolls his eyes and starts off down the long hall ahead of them. Brandon follows in Jessica's footsteps, stopping at the second floor while she goes all the way up to the third.

Minutes pass as the three explorers roam their assigned spaces, taking footage of every dusty corner and catching the sound of every creaking floorboard.

Up on the third floor, Jessica fights with a stubborn door. Finally, as she forces it open, it lets out a long creak that sounds to Jessica's ears almost like a baby's cry.

She pauses, a sudden vertigo washing over her. She puts her hand up to her forehead for a moment, closing her eyes until the room stops spinning.

When she opens her eyes, she gasps.

She's in the doorway of a large room which spans the length of the attic. A fire blazes in a small fireplace at the end of the room. Half a dozen old-fashioned hurricane lamps light the space with an amber glow.

Jessica closes her eyes, counts to ten. She makes it to eight before the cry cuts through the air. She opens her eyes, looks around frantically for the source of the sound.

There, in a dark and recessed part of the room, she spies the slatted sides of a crib, and standing in front of them, the dark silhouette of a man. Jessica takes a step backward, fear tracing fingers of ice up her spine. The cry comes again, loud enough to make Jessica's ears hurt. She drops her phone to the floor as she covers her ears with both hands.

It doesn't help. The cry pierces into her brain and she winces.

"Stop it," she says, then again, louder, "STOP IT!"

A low chuckle accompanies the baby's whimpers. Jessica narrows her eyes, gazing into the shadows around the crib. Yes, the shape of a man is there, with one arm disappearing down into the crib.

Jessica fumes with anger. "You're making that baby cry! Stop it! Stop hurting her!"

From the crib comes another wail, sharper and higher than before. Jessica lunges forward before she can think to stop herself.

The details of the man come into focus as she comes nearer: he's young, with a haughty set to his mouth and a strange fire in his eyes that ruin an otherwise handsome face.

Jessica tears her eyes away from the man to look in the crib. A bundle of blankets, a darker shape against the gloom, lies within. The man's arm disappears into that darkness. The arm tenses, and another wail slices through the air.

"Stop!" Jessica shouts, and she reaches into the crib and pulls out the bundle, strangely light. She pulls back the blankets as the man laughs again.

Inside is nothing but an old doll, one eye stuck shut and one staring lifelessly at the ceiling.

As Jessica stares, confused, at the doll, the cry comes again.

She raises her head slowly, fighting a voice inside her which screams at her to do exactly the opposite. Her eyes come to rest on the man's mouth, and she realizes with dawning horror that the sounds are coming from *him*.

She drops the bundle back into the crib and turns to run, but a cold hand clamps over her arm and holds her with an iron grip.

"Oh, no, pretty one," the man's voice purrs, his mouth against her ear, though she can feel no breath as he speaks. "I think I'll keep you here with me. You'll never leave, either."

"Jessica?" Brandon calls from the base of the stairs leading up to the third floor. He's getting impatient, irritated with her lack of response. He turns as Eddie's footsteps come up behind him.

"What is she *doing* up there?" Eddie asks. Brandon shakes his head in frustration and starts up the stairs to find her.

"Jessica?" he calls, and after a moment Eddie, too, ascends the stairs.

"Jessica?" they both shout, going through the one and only open door, shining their flashlights into every corner of the empty room that runs the length of the attic.

"That's so weird," Eddie says, as he turns to Brandon.

His foot steps down on something hard, something which cracks beneath his weight. He bends down and comes back up with Jessica's phone in his hand, the screen spiderwebbed with fractures.

"Jessica?" Brandon's voice is frantic now, annoyance turning to concern laced through with shots of fear. "Damn it! Where can she be? Jessica!"

The room remains empty, silent except for Brandon's own distraught voice, which echoes back to him in a sound like a baby's cry.

Up All Night

Marla Hemsworth knew what she knew, and what she knew was that someone was scoping out her house.

She'd heard the sounds: rustling in the bushes just outside her bedroom, steps of hard-soled boots on the sidewalk that ran around the side of the house.

She'd seen the evidence: footprints in the mud beside the back door, smudged fingerprints on the outside of the windows, a stack of cigarette butts behind the water meter.

Someone was outside her small clapboard house, all hours of the night, but she didn't know who and she didn't know why. Were they there to rob her? Murder her? Rape her? Kidnap one or both of her children? Was it someone she knew – maybe her ex-husband had sent a friend round to scare her? Was it a violent criminal, neighborhood kids playing jokes, or maybe a peeping Tom?

Marla Hemsworth knew what she knew, and what she knew was that she was scared.

She had called the police half a dozen times, but the man was always gone by the time they arrived. She showed them the footprints, the cigarettes, the fingerprints, but the officers just shook their heads and told her that unless the culprit was caught in the act, there was nothing much they could do.

She asked to have an officer assigned to her house for a few nights in hopes of catching the stalker. They said her case wasn't extreme enough to merit that.

She asked if they could send extra patrols to keep an eye on her street. They said they didn't have the manpower.

She asked what would happen if she shot the man if she saw him outside her house. They said she'd be the one charged, unless she could prove that the man was actually planning to commit a crime.

She asked how on earth she was supposed to prove that. They said *unless the man is actively trying to get into your house, you can't shoot him.*

She said that was good enough for her, and she settled in to wait.

Marla Hemsworth put her kids to bed in the dining room that night. At the center of the house, the dining room had no windows, no way for the mysterious stalker to see them or gain access to them without going through Marla first.

She wheeled Mary Jane's crib into one corner and set Billy up on a pallet in another. She tucked them both in and sang a few songs until the children drifted off, breaths deep and steady as they slept.

Then Marla Hemsworth sat down in the rocking chair in the living room, just a few feet away from her sleeping children. She draped a light summer quilt across her legs and laid her daddy's old hunting rifle across her knees. She made sure she could see her children clearly on one side, and the living room windows with the blinds only half-closed on the other. She settled in to wait.

The night was dark, but the yellow glow of a distant streetlamp cast just enough light to make the shadows of the trees visible against the windows. Now and then a breeze stirred the branches into motion, and far off in the distance flashes of heat lightning lit up the sky.

Marla sung to herself, hummed to herself, talked quietly to herself to keep herself awake, because Marla Hemsworth knew what she knew, and what she knew was that the moment she fell asleep the old creeper would be at her window, and she wasn't going to miss her chance.

Midnight came and went.

Just after one, Marla made a hurried trip to the bathroom, leaving the door open so as not to let her children out of her sight.

Just after two, she caught herself dozing and made herself get up and walk a few circles around the room, swinging her arms back and forth to get her blood pumping again.

Just after three, she heard the first sounds. Footsteps: a man, walking slowly up the sidewalk. He didn't seem to be trying to hide what he was doing at all, and what possible good reason could any man have for walking up her sidewalk at three in the morning?

Marla sat completely still, barely daring to breathe, as her eyes followed the sound of the footsteps: up the front walk, a turn at the porch, along the front wall, a turn at the corner, around to the side of the house and… they stopped just outside the window directly in front of her. He was there, on the other side of the wall, barely ten feet away.

Marla leaned as far back as she could in the chair and tucked her feet in under her, disappearing completely into the shadows.

She strained her eyes, peering through the slats of the blinds. Beyond the glass a quick flare of fire and then a dull red glow, the perfect round cherry of the man's cigarette. For a few moments Marla watched soundlessly as the stalker smoked. Every few seconds her eyes darted toward her children, peaceful and oblivious, and then shot back toward the window.

She sucked in a sharp breath as the man leaned against the window, cupping his hands around his eyes to peer inside. Marla prayed that he could not see her, that the shadows would continue to hide her until she was ready to do what she knew she had to do.

The man's silhouette pulled back from the window, and Marla breathed out.

Then he began to push at the window. Marla's heart pounded double-time in her chest as the man worked, shoving at the locked frame. A small grunt of effort and frustration sounded in his throat, and then the stalker renewed his efforts.

Marla made to stand, pulling away the quilt with her left hand, the rifle held tightly in her right. Her first step forward tangled in the blanket, making her stumble, her grip on the gun tightening as she tried to keep her balance. A thunderous boom shook the air around her, the floor vibrating as a bullet punctured the wood and buried itself in the crawl space beneath.

Marla let out a panicked yelp. The children stirred, Billy sitting up and looking around wildly, Mary Jane letting out a wail from her crib. Marla spared the children a moment's glance before turning her attention back to the window. The man had stopped pushing at the window but he stood there still, his shadow clear-cut as another flash of lighting lit the sky beyond.

He was backing away, panicked, Marla was sure, by the unexpected blast. She saw his head turn one way and then another, looking for the source of the sound.

He was leaving, he was moving away from the window.

She could not let him escape.

The words of the young police officer ran through Marla's brain: *unless he's actively trying to get into your house, you can't shoot him.*

Marla paced toward the window, her bare feet making no sound as she crossed the wooden floor. She could see the man better now, see the lines of his face, the buttons of his shirt, everything cast in amber by the streetlight's glow. He had backed away three feet now, back to the sidewalk. He was turning, turning to go, to get away, to escape.

Marla raised the gun and slid it between the slats of the blinds; she felt the tip of the barrel press against the glass. She braced herself and aimed just like her daddy had taught her to.

She pulled the trigger.

The glass shattered with a high-pitched squeal, shards flying straight out along the walls both inside and out. Again the deafening boom rolled through the small house, and the children's wails grew louder. Marla waited, listening, until she heard the sound that made her heart leap: a pain-filled moaning from just beyond the wall.

She chanced a look behind her just in time to see Billy peek cautiously around the doorframe. "Go back," she whispered to him, shooing him away with her free hand. "Go stay with your sister. Everything's going to be okay. I'll be back in just a minute."

Billy, eyes round in the darkness, nodded and crept across to his sister's crib, wrapping his arms around her and comforting her as well as he could.

Marla slipped on her old ratty house shoes and opened the front door. She walked through the night, along the sidewalk, in front of the bushes, around the corner. She stopped a safe distance away from a dark heap on the ground that she knew to be a man.

His face turned toward her, eyes blazing with hatred and pain. His hands were pressed against his chest, a bloom of fresh blood spreading across his shirt, black in the darkness.

Marla smiled. Right where she'd aimed. "You shot me, you damned bitch!" the man hissed through clenched teeth.

"You got just what you deserved," she said back to him, her voice quiet and calm, and then she got to work.

It took her the better part of an hour to do what needed doing.

First, she had to drag the man right up against the house. He moaned and groaned quite a bit during this part. By the time she hoisted his body up and halfway through the shattered window, he had ceased to make noise.

He had also stopped breathing.

Marla went back inside and surveyed her work. The man's front half hung through the window, his legs dangled against the wall outside. He wasn't moving. Blood still dripped from the left side of his chest, but the flow was much lighter now than it had been earlier.

Mary Jane had fallen back asleep in her crib, soothed by her brother's presence. Billy sat against the wall next to her, arms around his knees.

"You okay, Billy?" Marla said, and Billy nodded. "Okay then, you just give Mama one more minute, and I'll be done."

Marla went into her bedroom and changed from her blood-soaked nightgown into a clean one. She scrubbed her face and neck and arms in the bathroom until not a single speck of red remained. Then she balled up the bloody gown and wrapped the bloody shoes inside it, shoved both into a garbage bag, and tossed them down the basement stairs. She looked around, taking in the scene, and nodded.

Marla crouched down next to Billy and took him in her arms. "Did you see Mama shoot that man as he was coming through our window?" she asked him.

Billy looked up at her, sleep already reclaiming him, and nodded. "Yes, Mama. He was comin' through the window and you shooted him."

Marla stroked the boy's head a few times and then picked him up and took him to his own bed, tucking him in safely beneath the blankets. She then wheeled Mary Jane's crib back into the nursery, patting the baby as she went to keep her from waking.

Then Marla picked up the phone and called the police. It took them twenty minutes to arrive at her house, and she was glad to see the same handsome young officer who had told her what she needed to know just a few days prior.

Marla stood calmly as the police investigated the scene.

"You shot him, ma'am?" the young officer asked.

"Yes, sir, I did. I heard a noise and came running, with my daddy's shotgun in hand, and there he was, already halfway through the window. I was scared to death, officer, but I managed to shoot him and… I think, sir, that I might have killed him."

The officer looked at the dead man halfway through the window, then back at the young mother. She raised her eyes innocently to him and gave him a sad smile.

"Alright, ma'am. We'll get this whole mess cleaned up as quickly as we can and maybe you can get a little sleep before the sun comes up."

Marla smiled and dipped her head in appreciation.

The next day, Marla accepted the generosity of her neighbors as they offered to replace the broken window in her living room.

Everyone on the street knew what had happened by noon, and all were shocked by the turn of events and went out of their way to comfort and help the brave young mother.

That night, with a new window firmly in place and the bloodstains scrubbed from the floor, Marla tucked her children into their beds and then climbed into her own.

Marla Hemsworth knew what she knew, and what she knew was that anybody who thought they could harm her babies, well, they had just better think again.

Fiery Eyes and Bloody Bones

Zeke Blackwell stepped down off the school bus with a smile on his face. He took a few steps, turned, then watched the bus lumber off down the road.

He raised his hand in a parting wave and then, when he was sure the bus was far enough away that old Mr. Laramie, the driver, couldn't see it, he turned his hand around and flipped the bird, his middle finger jutting high up into the November sky.

Zeke chuckled and dropped his arm. He hiked his backpack up on his beefy shoulders and started off down the long dirt drive to the house where he lived with his grandmother.

Dead leaves, brown and paper-thin, scuttled before him as he walked. Zeke was happy, a dopey grin spreading beneath his wide cheeks and dark, piggish eyes. He was happy because this year his school had come up with the grand idea to let the kids have the entire week of Thanksgiving off, which meant that as he shuffled down the driveway that Friday afternoon, he had a full nine days of freedom stretching out ahead of him.

Zeke did an awkward, twirling dance as he ascended the old wooden steps to the front porch. He let the screen door slam behind him as he entered the dim cabin. The trees of the surrounding forest had crept closer and closer each year until they cast the entire house in shade no matter what time of day it was.

Inside, the house was sparsely furnished and what few furnishings it did have had to be at least fifty years old. A ratty orange couch and a threadbare recliner sat in the small living room, with an old console TV that only picked up three channels, and that only if you managed to wiggle the old foil-wrapped rabbit-ear antenna in just the right way.

Two doorways opened off the living room, one to the left and one toward the back of the house. Zeke swerved through the one on the left, entering the small hallway that led to the two tiny bedrooms and an even tinier bathroom.

He banged into the back bedroom, the door slamming against the wall as he entered, the doorknob fitting perfectly into the hole it had smashed there months ago when Zeke first took up residence at Granny's.

Zeke kicked his shoes off under the bed, threw his jacket into the closet floor. From the depths of his bag, he pulled the snacks he had stolen from his classmates during lunch; he hid them in his dresser drawers and dropped the bag in the middle of the floor. In his stocking feet he padded back through the living room and into the kitchen, all yellow linoleum and ancient appliances.

Granny was there, as she was most days, stirring something in a big pot on the old stove. She looked up wearily as Zeke entered, her eyes roaming over the great solid bulk of him.

She'd once remarked to her own son, Zeke's father, that if the boy didn't stop eating so much he'd be too big to fit through the door by the time he finished high school – if he managed to do that.

Zeke had come to live with his granny that summer, at the age of thirteen, when his father finally managed to land his dream job, doing long-haul trucking back and forth across the country, conveniently gone for days or even weeks at a time.

It was no bother to Zeke, who had never known his mother and never cared much for his father. Granny's small cabin was just as good as any of the tiny apartments he'd ever lived in with his dad, and the food was a thousand times better, so he had no complaints.

If Granny had any complaints, aside from Zeke's insatiable appetite, she kept them to herself.

Zeke sat down at the old Formica table, once red but now faded to a sickly pinkish-brown that reminded him of the color of vomit. He reached across and wrapped both arms around the plate of cookies that sat in the center of the table, pulling it toward him and then shoving an entire cookie into his mouth in one gluttonous bite.

Zeke ate nine cookies, and then asked what was for dinner.

Granny sighed.

The next morning dawned crisp and cool, fog rising up from the hollers and drifting like ghosts between the trees. Zeke was up and dressed and out of the house by nine, having eaten six waffles and stuffed two more in his jacket pocket to eat as he walked.

He had just made it to the bottom of the porch steps when Granny stepped out behind him, pointing the wooden spoon she held in her hand at him like a warning as she reminded him for the hundredth time to be careful and not wander past the markers.

"Yes, Granny," Zeke sighed, but as he turned away from her he rolled his eyes.

She was always, always on to him about not going past those damn markers. He hadn't disobeyed her on this point – not yet – but he did like to sit on the old sawed-off stumps that separated the "safe" part of Granny's mountain property from the "unsafe."

He went there now, chewing his mouthful of waffle slowly to make it last longer.

It took twenty minutes to reach the markers. Zeke was sweating by the time he got there, despite the briskness of the November morning. He unzipped his jacket and dropped his backpack to the ground.

Earlier that morning, he'd dumped out all his schoolbooks and papers and the layer of trash that had accumulated in the bottom of the bag, making a messy pile of it all in one corner of his room.

He'd then repacked the bag with snacks and a couple cans of orange soda from the fridge. He pulled out one of the cans now and popped it open, sucking down the entire fizzy contents in under a minute.

Zeke wiped his mouth on his sleeve, crumpled the can in his fist. He thought about chucking it off into the woods but then thought better of it.

Granny never came out here, as far as he knew, but she did have ways of knowing things she had no business knowing, so Zeke thought better of it and dropped the crumpled can back into his bag.

He settled down onto the stump he'd come to think of as his own and looked around. Between here and the house the forest was more open, the trees spaced fifteen feet apart, little patches of grass growing up in the sunny spots between.

Behind him, in the part of the property he was *never, ever to go in, no matter what*, it was darker, the trees so close together in some spots that Zeke's bulky frame would never manage to squeeze through.

Separating the two sections, stretching out – for miles, if what Granny said was true – in both directions was the line of stumps.

Each was about two feet high, and each had two holes drilled into it through which long lines of rusty barbed wire were strung. It was not a fence that would keep anyone out or in; Granny simply said it was the boundary and so it was.

Zeke had come out here many times over the summer. A couple of days stuck inside the cabin with only Granny and the local news channel for company had been enough for him; he'd gone out to explore and found this spot, a spot where he could gaze into the dark shady coolness of the property beyond but still see, just barely, the top of Granny's chimney over the next rise.

Since school started he hadn't been out much, and things looked so different that he simply sat and stared for a while.

Months before, the forbidden part of the property had been dark and mysterious; now, with autumn's winds having emptied the treetops of their cover, the woods were lighter, brighter, less ominous.

A carpet of leaves spread across the forest floor. Everything was the same brown color: the dirt, the leaves, the tall tree trunks reaching toward the blue-gray sky above.

Zeke sat, peering around, eyes roaming from tree to tree, taking in this newly opened line of sight into the world beyond. He scanned from left to right and back again and then…–

He stopped, let his eyes trail back a few trees. There was something – just there, just barely within range of his squinting eyes – a line that didn't belong.

It looked almost like… like the roof of a house?

Zeke peered forward, frustrated. He needed to see it better. He stood, put a hand over his eyes to block out the sun that was now almost directly overhead. It still wasn't enough. He took a step forward, jumped back with a yelp.

The barbed wire caught in his jeans, and they pulled free with a ripping sound as he twisted and stumbled, landing on his backside on the wrong side of the barrier.

A rapid-fire drumbeat thrummed through his heart, and he stood and scrambled back over to the safe side, careful this time to step high over the wire.

He bent down, as far as he could with his full belly in the way, and looked at the damage. A line of beaded blood curved across his shin, accompanied by a painful stinging.

That was the least of Zeke's problems though, as far as he was concerned. He could wash off the blood and put on a Band-Aid in the bathroom and Granny would never know.

Hiding the three-inch tear in his new blue jeans would not be so easy.

Zeke stood up suddenly as the sound of a ringing bell pealed out across the hollow. That was Granny, letting him know that lunch was ready. Zeke zipped up his bag, slung it over his shoulder, and headed home.

Granny was in the kitchen when he came in, so he went quietly around to the front door in hopes of avoiding her.

He hurried into the hall, calling out, "Just a minute! Bathroom!" He rummaged around in his chest-of-drawers for a pair of sweatpants, then went into the bathroom.

He stripped off his jeans, cleaned the blood from his leg – it was barely enough of a scratch to bother with – and pulled on the sweats. He tossed his jeans into the pile of dirty laundry in his room. He'd deal with them later.

As Zeke and Granny sat together in the kitchen eating lunch, they heard the first patter of raindrops on the tin roof. Zeke raised his eyes to the kitchen window and looked out as the sky lost all its blue and the clouds opened up.

He dropped his gaze back to his plate and sighed. There'd be no going back out to the woods today.

There was an old black-and-white cowboy movie on TV that afternoon and Zeke sat on the ancient couch, staring at the screen without paying much attention, while Granny drifted in and out of sleep in the recliner.

The rain still fell steadily when the movie went off, and Zeke, with a rush of courage born of boredom, turned to face his granny with a question on his lips.

"Granny?" he asked.

"Yes, child?" she answered, her eyes opening slowly to gaze at him in the low light.

"I was out in the woods today, just at the boundary, and I thought I saw, way back in the woods… a building of some kind? A house maybe? What would that be?"

Granny sat up straighter in her chair. Her eyes looked wild.

"You tell me the truth now, Zeke. You been going out in those woods where you don't belong? You been passing the boundary?"

Zeke shook his head. That one moment earlier today when he'd stumbled over the barbed wire didn't count.

Granny stared at him for a moment before speaking.

"Now you listen to me, and you listen close, Zeke. Are you listening?"

Zeke could tell from the sound of her voice that she wasn't going to tell him anything he wanted to hear, but he kept quiet and nodded.

"You stay out of those woods and you stay away from that house and don't you never ever under any circumstances step foot inside it. You understand me?"

There was a fierceness in her eyes and a quaver to her voice that made Zeke realize that she was actually afraid of something out there, in those woods or in that house.

"Do you understand?" she demanded.

Zeke nodded, but spoke anyway: "But what is that house? What's so bad about it? What's in there?"

Granny stood to her feet, wobbling a bit on her ancient legs. She pointed a gnarled finger at Zeke and spittle flew from her mouth as she shouted.

"You just stay away, child! Just stay away! Nothing good in that house for a boy like you! Nothing good for a child with no manners and lying ways! Nothing there but fiery eyes and bloody bones! Now… now go to your room!"

Granny collapsed back into her chair and turned away from him. Stunned, Zeke stood up and walked past her toward his bedroom.

As he passed through into the hallway, he heard something that sounded very much like a sob.

Zeke lay on his bed staring at the ceiling for the rest of the afternoon. Granny knocked softly at the door at dinnertime, but when he came to the kitchen there was only one place set at the table and Granny was wiping her hands on her apron and telling him that she was going to bed early and to wash up good after himself when he was finished eating.

It was dark by six o'clock and the rain, though it had lessened in intensity, still pinged against the metal roof as Zeke sat by himself out on the porch watching the last of the light fade around him.

He'd eaten three bowls of stew, and then dumped his dishes in the sink for Granny to deal with in the morning.

He was troubled by Granny's words, by the thought of "fiery eyes and bloody bones," but more so by her calling him a child with no manners and lying ways. He felt insulted, indignant whenever he let his brain linger too long on this thought.

By eight o'clock, he had decided that Granny was an even crazier old loon than he'd previously thought.

By nine o'clock, he had worked himself up into a righteous indignation over her insults.

By ten o'clock, he had made up his mind and was sneaking around his room quietly in the dark, packing a flashlight and an extra sweatshirt and some spare snacks he'd had squirreled away in his desk drawers into his backpack.

He waited until he was on the front porch to pull his shoes on, not daring to risk the sound of footsteps within the house.

Zeke pulled the door closed behind him, gently, until he heard the clear click that told him it had latched properly. Then he set off into the night.

He walked quickly, much more quickly than he'd ever walked this same path in the daytime. He walked so quickly, in fact, that he was surprised by the stump-and-wire boundary when he came upon it.

Zeke stopped for a moment. He tugged at his pants and adjusted the straps of his bag and looked all around himself in the pale moonlight.

He gazed back toward the cabin for a few minutes, imagining his grandmother sleeping soundly in her bed, snoring that strange little whistling snore that he found so funny.

For a moment he was shot through with something that felt suspiciously like love, but it was overridden immediately by a feeling of resentful anger. He'd show her. He'd go out to that house and bring something back to prove that he'd been there, and she'd have to admit how stupid her rules were and how brave and good he was.

Zeke gave a resolute nod and stepped over the wire into the close-grown trees.

It took him far longer than he'd anticipated to reach the old house, and a few times he wondered if he'd started off in the wrong direction altogether, if perhaps he was simply wandering further and further into the acres of woodland that filled the hollow and rose up the sloping sides of the Ozark mountains beyond.

For two hours he trudged, his shoes and socks soaked through, his cheeks red from the cold, before he finally saw it. Up ahead and a little to the left, he spied the roofline of the house he had spotted earlier from the boundary.

Zeke made his way through the trees toward the house, and as he came closer he realized that the house was actually two stories high, built down in a depression within the land so that from far away only the top half could be seen.

It was tall and skinny, maybe ten feet wide across the front and stretching twenty feet back, and it leaned slightly, first one way and then the other, and Zeke thought briefly of that old nursery rhyme about the crooked man who lived in a crooked house.

Gathered all around the small hollow in which the house stood was a thick layer of fog, thicker than Zeke had ever seen before, so thick he had a sudden fear that he would not be able to pass through it, that it was a solid presence which he would bounce off of should he try to run into it.

He descended slowly down the steep banks of the hollow, slipping a bit on the dead, wet grass but managing to stay upright all the way to the bottom. The fog stood before him like a wall, and he stretched his hand out toward it tentatively.

Zeke breathed a sigh of relief as his hand passed harmlessly through the mist. It was cold and damp but that wasn't so strange.

He went forward, toward the vague shadowy structure in front of him.

The fog closed in around him on all sides, and Zeke forced himself to take slow, steadying breaths as he walked, his arms out in front of him.

His legs found the house before he did, and he cursed under his breath as he banged his bandaged shin against an old board that must be the bottom step of the porch. Carefully, he ascended one step, two, three, and then his feet found a wide expanse of rugged floorboards which must be the porch proper.

He shuffled forward until his hands found the rough wood of the door, and he ran his fingers down it, ready at any moment for a splinter, until his fingers closed around an old bronze doorknob.

He turned the knob and pushed.

The door opened an inch at most. Zeke huffed out a plume of smoky breath and shoved against it with his shoulder. It moved a little more and then snagged again on the uneven boards of the room within.

After three hard shoves, Zeke had managed an opening just large enough to squeeze his broad shoulders and thick stomach through.

Inside the house, all was dark.

All was quiet.

Zeke looked around. There were windows on three sides, the thick fog pressing against what remained of the broken glass but coming no further, as if nature herself knew better than to trespass within these rotting walls.

Zeke swung his bag around in front of him and pulled out his flashlight. It made a perfect white oval of light on the floor in front of him. He turned in a circle, inspecting the place where he stood.

The floor, though old and rough and uneven, looked sturdy enough. He raised the light to the walls and passed it slowly over the faded wallpaper. The room was completely empty.

On the back wall was a doorway, and Zeke walked slowly toward it. He expected a kitchen, like the one through the back doorway at Granny's house, but instead he found another empty room.

Well, no… not empty.

His flashlight beam dropped and illuminated an old mattress in the middle of the floor. A heap of blankets, colorless in the darkness, was shoved to one side, like someone had just awakened, thrown the blankets off, and walked away somewhere.

Along one wall of this room was a staircase leading up to the second floor. Zeke stood for a long time at the bottom of the stairs, looking up, his flashlight beam playing over the bottom half dozen or so steps.

Beyond that the light did not reach and all was in shadow.

Zeke's hand rested on the old newel post. He lifted one foot up to the first stair, then the other. The wood creaked with such loud ferocity at this intrusion that he quickly stepped back down.

Zeke looked once more around the room he stood in. Yes. He'd stay here. He wasn't afraid of all those old backwoods bogeymen that Granny believed in, but he understood the laws of gravity well enough to know that falling through a rotten step would not be pleasant.

Zeke inspected the mattress. It was old and a few springs poked through, but it would have to do. He sat down on it and opened his bag.

He took off his coat, pulled on his extra sweatshirt, and put the coat back on over it, protection against the cold and damp. Then he helped himself to a few Twinkies and cursed himself for not bringing anything to drink.

A glance at his watch told him that it was now nearly one o'clock in the morning, and his eyes suddenly felt heavy. He shook out the blankets that were piled on the mattress, making sure that no beetles or spiders or snakes had sought warmth within.

It occurred to him that it was strange that no critters were taking refuge in this house, which was hardly perfect but would surely be better than the cold, wet autumn woods outside.

He did not have time to ponder this strange observation. His eyes closed and his body relaxed against the protesting springs of the mattress, and he slept.

Beneath him, beneath the mattress, beneath the floorboards, something shifted. A thing which had long been asleep stirred itself into wakefulness.

It stretched out ancient limbs in its cellar sanctum and opened eyes which lit the dark space around it with a red and fiery glow.

It lifted its pale head and sniffed the air. Above the odors of damp and rot and mildew and dirt drifted a high and unmistakable scent, the scent which has called forth bogeyman since the creation of the world: the scent of a naughty child.

Zeke slept, and as he slept, he dreamed. In his dreams were awful, unpleasant things, sounds and smells and shapes that failed to resolve into anything recognizable but which morphed over and over from one almost-nightmare to another.

Suddenly he shot upright, looking about frantically, some forgotten shout or cry for help still forming in his throat.

It took a moment for him to recall where he was.

He pressed the button on his watch and the glowing numbers told him he'd been asleep for two hours. He sighed and laid back on the mattress, wishing he had a pillow.

His mouth was still dry and had an unpleasant taste inside.

He closed his eyes, determined to go back to sleep until the sun rose.

Something thumped the floor beneath him.

Zeke's eyes shot open. He lay still, letting his gaze roam around the bare walls, listening intently.

Thump.

This time the floor shook with the sound.

Something is banging on the floor from underneath, Zeke thought. *But how? Is there a basement? A cellar? A crawl space?*

He hadn't seen any sort of access to a space below the floor, but he shot to his feet as an idea occurred to him. He grabbed a corner of the mattress and pulled, shoving it up against the far wall.

There, just beneath where he had been sleeping, a trap door was set into the floor, with an old iron bolt to keep it locked.

Zeke knelt on the floor beside the door, not yet daring to touch it, just looking. He waited, and listened, but the thumping sound did not come again.

With shaking hands, Zeke grasped the iron bolt and pulled. It moved slowly at first, then slid back so quickly that Zeke fell backward onto his ample backside.

He grasped the iron pull-ring and lifted. The door was solid, but not too heavy, and Zeke swung it up with ease.

He looked down into blackness. Careful to keep his distance from the gaping hole, Zeke skirted around to where his bag lay, shoved between the mattress and the wall, and pulled out his flashlight.

The floorboards were rough and gritty beneath his palms as he crawled close to the hole and shone the light down into the darkness.

There was nothing so scary there, just a small cellar, dirt-lined, dirt-floored, smelling faintly of mildew. The space seemed to go on a ways beneath the floor, and Zeke, mustering up his courage, dropped himself in feet-first.

The cellar was only about four feet deep, he reckoned, and he had to crouch down to fit his head inside.

Zeke swept the flashlight back and forth. A few worm-ends wiggled in the walls; on the packed-earth floor he could just make out the gleam of a few tarnished bottle caps.

There was something at the far end, a shapeless pile of debris stacked against the back wall. Zeke crawled toward it, his shoulders scraping the walls on either side as he went forward, one hand awkwardly holding the flashlight.

His empty hand touched something slightly wet, sticky and gummy and strangely warm, and he pulled back in disgust. He pointed the flashlight at the spot and leaned closer to examine it. A glob of dark red liquid, thick like congealed blood, was smeared across the floor. Stuck within it were several strands of hair.

Zeke's nose wrinkled and he scooted back a few inches. He turned his head toward the spot where he'd entered the cellar, just to make sure it was still there. A pale shaft of moonlight shone through the trapdoor.

Zeke swallowed, nodded to himself, turned away from the moonlight, and crept on, carefully avoiding the streak of blood on the ground.

A few more feet brought him close enough to pick out the distinct shapes of the things which were piled against the wall.

Zeke's heart did a backflip in his chest.

They were bones, bones of all kinds and sizes, leg bones and rib cages and long skinny finger bones, and here and there shone the smooth rounded dome of a human skull. Zeke froze, eyes wide and flashlight trembling in his hand.

Some of the bones still had bits of decaying flesh attached to them, some were striped with blood. More hair – some in individual strands and some in larger clumps – was stuck to the skulls and smeared along the bones.

As Zeke stared at the pile, his brain refusing to comprehend what he was seeing, refusing to process any logical sort of reasoning for it, the femurs and ribcages and skulls began to shift.

From the center of the pile the bones began to fall inward, as if sucked back by some strange force, until a cavity formed, an abyss of darkness. Zeke held his breath.

A strangled cry rose and died in his throat as two skeletal hands reached up out of the opening, pushing the bones aside as they widened the gap, and something began to pull itself up and out of the pile.

The hands groped, then long, pale arms appeared; a head came next, just the top of a skull at first, long stringy hair stuck in bloody patches along its crown.

The skull lifted, and the face looked out at Zeke as he cowered in the confines of the cellar.

The thing opened its eyes and fire seemed to dance within them, painting the cellar walls in dancing reds and oranges. Blood dripped from the eye sockets and sharp teeth gnashed as the creature pulled itself further from its macabre hiding place.

Zeke's primal instincts kicked in, overriding his brain, his logic, his fear; he scooted backward along the cellar floor on his backside, hands behind him and legs kicking out in front in a bizarre impression of a crab.

His back slammed hard into a solid wall of dirt and he looked up into the moonlight that filled the room above him. He stood, legs trembling, and hoisted himself clumsily from the hole.

From within the cellar came the clattering sound of many bones falling over and over each other, and firelight crept slowly along the walls toward where Zeke stood watching from above.

He grabbed the trapdoor, meaning to slam it closed and bolt it tight, but the door, so easy to move just a few minutes earlier, now felt as if it weighed a thousand pounds. Zeke could not budge it even a fraction of an inch.

His gaze darted to the doorway. His heart clenched as his eyes met nothing but solid wall.

The doorway to the front room was gone, completely gone.

A wet, rattling breath echoed out from the cellar and a long, bony hand stretched out across the floor just beneath the trapdoor.

Zeke looked around, frantic for a means of escape. His eyes fell on the rickety old staircase. He had no choice. He ran for it, feet pounding, wood groaning, the entire house swaying with the force of his footsteps.

At the top, the stairs opened up into one wide room which ran the narrow length of the house. Zeke ran a circle around the room, desperate, seeking a way out which he knew would not be there.

Then he paused, for his eyes had finally taken in the thing which spread across the long wall.

Painted across the bare wooden boards was a figure, enormous, stretching for fifteen or twenty feet. It was done in the chalky whiteness of bone dust, patterned with long streaks of dark red blood.

A monstrous creature, with red flaming eyes and sharp teeth and impossibly thin arms and legs.

The drawing – the painting – the picture, whatever it was, showed the skull of the creature up close, the full height of the room, with arms bent to either side and legs trailing off in the distance, just as if the creature were about to crawl right through the wall and into the room with him.

Zeke backed away from the drawing. He slid along the opposite wall, splinters digging into the thick flesh of his back. It was coming, he could hear it: slowly crossing the room below, then the creak of the stairs, the thing's footsteps like the clink of old bones.

And then the voice:

"I'm coming for you, Ezekiel Blackwell. I'm on the first *step."*

Zeke's legs went out from under him and he huddled in the far corner.

"You've been a naughty boy, Ezekiel Blackwell. I'm on the second *step."*

The voice was the sound of a dying man's groan, the sound of a swarm of angry bees, the sound of thunder right after a lightning flash.

"Nothing good here for you in this house, Ezekiel Blackwell. I'm on the third *step."*

The familiar words cut through his fear: the exact words that Granny had said.

"Nothing good here for a boy with no manners, Ezekiel Blackwell. I'm on the fourth *step."*

Zeke's face was wet with tears.

"Nothing good here for lying children. I'm on the fifth *step."*

Zeke's mind raced, frantically, trying to remember how many steps there were.

"Nothing good here for naughty children. I'm on the sixth *step."*

Zeke could hear the wet, rattling breath now as the thing climbed closer.

"Naughty children must be punished, Ezekiel Blackwell. I'm on the seventh *step."*

Zeke's hands covered his face, terrified eyes peering out through the cracks in his fingers.

"Are you a naughty child, Ezekiel Blackwell? I'm on the eighth *step."*

No-no-no, Zeke's mouth formed the shape of the words but no sounds came out.

"You are very, very naughty, Ezekiel Blackwell. I'm on the ninth *step."*

Zeke could see the flickering of firelight at the top of the stairs now, the long shadow of the creature as it came closer.

"Nothing good in this house for naughty children. I'm on the tenth *step."*

Zeke felt a warmth in his crotch and a trickle down his leg.

"Nothing good here for boys like you, Ezekiel Blackwell... I'm on the eleventh *step."*

It was almost to the top. A pale hand appeared on the wall next to the stairs.

"Nothing good at all ... I'm on the twelfth *step."*

And then the thing was in the room with him.

It stretched to its full height, its head brushing the ceiling. The body, the limbs were impossibly long; damp, glistening skin stretched taut over knobby bones, skin so pale that it seemed to shine; long streaks of blood smeared across arms, legs, ribs.

The face lifted and the blazing eyes turned their heated glare directly upon Zeke's cowering form.

The creature's mouth opened, all sharp teeth and dark chasm. Its voice filled the room though its mouth did not form speech, as if the words escaped from somewhere deep in its belly.

"Nothing good in this house for naughty children like you, Ezekiel Blackwell. Nothing here but fiery eyes and bloody bones!"

And the thing flew across the room toward him, and Zeke threw up his arms in hopeless defense, and the heat of the creature's stare washed over him so that he cried out in pain.

Zeke woke up, sweating, reeking of his own urine, gasping for breath.

He scurried off the old mattress and into a corner of the room, still clutching the soiled blankets to his chest.

He stayed there for an interminable time, breathing heavily, swallowing back the bile that rose in his throat, tears drying in salt tracks down his cheeks.

Outside, in the woods, an owl let out a mournful cry and Zeke jumped at the sound.

He stood until his limbs went stiff with shaking, and then numb, and then when feeling came back to them and he could breathe normally again, he dropped the blankets and approached the mattress with a feeling which was a mixture of disbelief and dread.

He picked up his bag, shoved his flashlight inside; he even picked up the crinkly plastic wrappers of the Twinkies he'd eaten earlier.

He stood staring at the mattress, wanting more than anything to leave this place, to run back to the safety of Granny's house and Granny herself, to apologize to her for every time he'd lied or talked back or stolen food from the kitchen, but something held him there, some morbid curiosity that said he could not leave until he had checked beneath the mattress, just to be sure.

Zeke shoved at the mattress with his foot, moving it across the floor little by little. His heart jumped when he saw the outline of the trapdoor in the pale pre-dawn light.

It's nothing, he told himself, his voice a murmuring whisper. *It's just a cellar door. You probably felt it through the mattress or something and dreamed about it. There's nothing really down there. It was just a dream.*

He knelt on the floor, grasped the iron bolt in both hands.

Please, please, don't let there be anything down there, please, I swear I'll be good from now on. I swear it. I won't be naughty anymore. I'll be good, I'll be good, I promise.

He pulled back the bolt. It slid with heavy thud.

He stuck a finger through the iron ring and took a deep breath.

He spoke aloud, a whisper to whatever gods might be listening. "Please let there be nothing there. I promise I'll be good from now on."

He lifted the door.

A blast of heat washed over him as the bright dancing light of a blazing fire made him throw an arm up over his eyes. From deep within the cellar came the sound of a thousand bones falling over and over each other, and a voice like thunder, like bees, like dying, rumbled up over it all.

"Too late, Ezekiel Blackwell, too late."

BLOSSOM

Harrison County Gazette
February 16, 1896

WE MUST END THIS EVIL
by Temperance Noble

Another tragic incident has occurred which illustrates once more the dire need for Harrison to become a DRY COUNTY.

This reporter has interviewed multiple sources and put together this awful timeline of the shocking events:

Around two o'clock yesterday afternoon, Tumley resident Mrs. Vera Calhoun left the small residence she shares with her husband, Hank Calhoun, and their young daughter, for an afternoon visit with her mother, Mrs. Grace

Henley. Mrs. Henley, we are told, lives about a mile outside the town of Tumley, just the other side of the Bright River. Mrs. Calhoun states that she has made the trek to her mother's residence and back during her daughter's afternoon nap many times before without incident.

On this particular afternoon, however, Mrs. Calhoun was delayed in returning. According to Mrs. Calhoun's own testimony, corroborated by several witnesses, she put her five-year-old daughter, Blossom, down for a nap, sure that she would return before the child awoke as usual, and left the rooms the family rent over Widmark's General Store just after two o'clock. Mr. Calhoun was away from the home at the time.

Mrs. Calhoun reached her mother's residence around two-thirty and stayed until four o'clock, meaning to return home by four-thirty, before Blossom awoke and before darkness fell. Mrs. Calhoun, however, was delayed at the bridge crossing the Bright River as a wagon traveling over the road had overturned and blocked the path. Mrs. Calhoun did her best to help gather the traveling family's belongings while they waited for men from town to come and help right the wagon and untangle the horses.

Back in the Calhoun residence, five-year-old Blossom awoke. One can only imagine the fear and confusion the child must have felt to awaken alone in a room growing dim with the winter twilight. One can imagine that she must have cried out for her mother, her father, for anyone to come and care for her. The horror of it strikes directly to this reporter's heart, dear readers.

Witnesses Carl and Mary Tetlinger, who were walking along Main Street around five-thirty in the evening, report a strange and troubling sight: little Blossom making her way cautiously down the outer staircase from her family's lodgings to the wooden sidewalk below. Mrs. Tetlinger reports that Blossom paused for a moment at the bottom of the stairs, suckling at her own fingers as she gazed around. The child then seemed to get her bearings and to spot her destination.

And what a destination it was, readers.

Blossom reportedly made her way down the sidewalk and across the dusty, packed earth of Tumley's main thoroughfare, straight to the door of that most hideous and unsavory of establishments, Correy's Saloon, known locally as the Gin Palace.

The child paused for the briefest of moments, then pushed on the swinging doors and entered.

Here we rely on the testimonies of saloon patron George Cardinal and barmaid Tessie Garr.

We know that the little girl stepped into the saloon. We know that she looked around the room, seeming mesmerized momentarily by the many lights cast upon the walls by lanterns shining through the colored bottles of liquor. We know that she then spotted her own father, Hank Calhoun, sitting at a table in the back corner. We know from several witnesses that Mr. Calhoun had been sitting in this same spot for most of the day, drinking. We know, in fact, that Mr. Calhoun spent almost all of his evenings and weekends in the saloon.

Here we interject with a short statement from Mrs. Grace Henley, Mrs. Calhoun's mother and little Blossom's grandmother:

"Hank Calhoun was a sorry, good-for-nothing excuse for a man. He was drunk all the time he wasn't at work, and even sometimes when he was there. His employer, Jim Garrison of Garrison's Lumber, really only kept him on out of pity for his wife and child. Hank would often come stumbling up the stairs to their rented rooms above the general store, weaving and swaying and falling all over himself. My daughter, Vera, did her best to keep herself and the child out of his way. She told me of one time when Hank came home even more drunk than usual, calling for his wife and baby and then berating Vera and calling her all sorts of ungodly names. Vera told me she just held little Blossom close against her while Hank ranted and raved, throwing things about the room and even kicking the baby's chair into the wall and breaking it before he stormed into the bedroom and collapsed onto the bed. He was a worthless piece of scum, and I begged my daughter many times to leave him, to come back home and bring Blossom with her. But she was stubborn, my Vera, and she loved the man, fool that she was. And now, and now…."

Here Mrs. Henley was unable to go on speaking, breaking into sobs and excusing herself.

Back to the time of last night's incident:

Little Blossom, upon recognizing her father, went toward him, her face alight with a smile that only the truly innocent can show. Our witnesses, Mr. Cardinal and Miss Garr, both confirm the words that the child spoke:

"Oh Papa! I thought if I came I would find you, and I is so glad you is here."

Mr. Cardinal, who was seated close to Mr. Calhoun, states that Blossom then went on to remark wonderingly about the lights and the music within the saloon, and then to ask her father to come home and fix her some supper, saying, "Blossom wants something to eat."

What happened next is truly horrible and depraved, dear readers. Those of you with weak constitutions may wish to stop reading.

Mr. Calhoun stared at his daughter, stared through the bleary-eyed haze of the deeply inebriated, stared as though he did not recognize this innocent creature standing before him, looking beseechingly up into his face and requesting her dinner.

Mr. Calhoun stood. He grasped the back of the chair next to him and raised it above him. Then, as his small child looked on with incomprehension and the other saloon patrons watched with dawning horror, Mr. Calhoun, like a man possessed, brought the chair down with one fierce and striking blow upon the back, neck, and head of his own child.

The child dropped to the floor, her body trembling in what our own Dr. Waring states were probably a series of small seizures brought on by the sudden damage caused to her brain.

Mr. Calhoun, shocked out of his drunken stupor by the shouts and gasps of the people around him, looked suddenly upon his child with clearing eyes. The truth of what he'd just done seemed to strike him (so say the witnesses), and he bent quickly and lifted the child, holding her to his chest and letting out what

Miss Garr, the barmaid, calls "a groan that the devil might pity."

The child, all witnesses report, looked up at her father for the briefest of moments. Her lips trembled as if to speak once more, then her body went limp in her father's arms as her innocent soul ascended to the Lord above.

Within moments, Sheriff Todd was on the scene. Hank Calhoun was taken immediately into custody. Little Blossom Calhoun's body was lifted and carried three doors down to Doc Waring's place, where he pronounced her undeniably dead.

Vera Calhoun was then seen running down the stairs from her family's lodgings, shouting Blossom's name frantically and asking every person on the street if they had seen her daughter. She had returned home too late. Far too late, readers.

Sheriff Todd says that Hank Calhoun will hang on Friday morning. In a direct quote, he says:

"He must hang, the only proper payment for the deed he has done. It's a terrible thing, just terrible. Only a fiend or a madman could murder his own child like this."

When this reporter, your own Temperance Noble, asked the sheriff if Mr. Correy, proprietor of Correy's Saloon, would be held at all responsible for the crimes that occurred due to the imbibing of that poison which he so generously provides to the men of our county, Sheriff Todd stated that Mr. Correy would face no criminal charges, because "after all, he has a license to sell."

God pity Vera Calhoun and sweet innocent Blossom Calhoun, and all the poor women and children who fall prey to this most vile and vicious of enemies!

God help us all, citizens of Harrison County, if we continue to let these liquors be sold and consumed within our boundaries. God help us, if we turn a blind eye to the harm caused by this consumption. The men of our county are held tightly with that grasp of that juggernaut, Rum, and all his assorted cousins: Whiskey, Brandy, Beer, and the like. We must wake up and see the damage these alcohols wreak upon our citizens, our families, our county! We must say No! We must say Enough! We must Vote! We must declare that Harrison County cares about its women, its children, and yes, even its men, and that we want no part of the evils that alcohol brings!

The Golden Arm

Lawrence Hanover considered himself a gift. With his dashing good looks, charming smile, impeccable grooming, fine manners, and ability to carry on an interesting and intelligent conversation with anyone who found themselves lucky enough to linger in his presence, he was – in his own mind, at least – the perfect man.

He found it somewhat vexing, therefore, that no woman seemed to want him.

No woman good enough for him, anyway.

He had worked his way through all the blushing maidens in the county in which he lived, yet none of these sufficed. (Though, admittedly, on occasion, some would have sufficed quite nicely, except that they clearly had no taste for the finer things in life, namely Lawrence himself.)

When he had exhausted the available prospects within a day's ride of his family home, Lawrence struck out for further, greener pastures.

He left his parents' house at the age of twenty-one. He did not return until the age of twenty-five.

In the intervening years, Lawrence courted, cajoled, and attempted to woo maidens of every shape, size, age, and coloring. He delivered roses, scraps of poetry, and lace handkerchiefs to ladies young and old, thick and thin, tall and short, blonde, brunette, red-haired. With each courtship, Lawrence's heart would swell, his pulse race, his mind fill with the imagined happiness that particular young lass could bestow upon his life. But, as the days passed, Lawrence's feelings would change, soured by such objectionable discoveries as a crooked tooth, a mole behind the ear, a strand of hair already showing silvered gray among a mane of raven strands.

This woman had hands too large, that one a laugh too loud. A quaint slip of a girl seemed perfect until he discovered the horror that she ate three *full* meals every day! Some were too brash, some too quiet. One was too attached to her own family; others were so unattached that Lawrence felt there must be some defect in them which made their families shun them.

And of course, those finest of young ladies – they of unquestionable breeding and physical perfection, blooming in grace and well-versed in the quiet subservience all loving maidens should bestow upon their suitors, these seemed somehow and for some reason utterly unattainable, turning up their pert little noses and gazing upon Lawrence with shrewd judgment in their sparkling eyes.

All in all, Lawrence spent a rather miserable four years.

He had nearly given up his search, ready to return home, dejected and alone, when he chanced to pass a night in a roadside inn, perhaps two days' ride from his ancestral manse.

The proprietor of this inn was a loud, burly fellow by the name of Burris; his wife was just as loud and at least twice as wide as he. Together they kept a clean but merry business, with good food and soft beds.

Lawrence had partaken of this fine food and was just gathering his coat and gulping down the last few sips of his ale when he saw her.

The great room of the inn had emptied out. The chairs sat empty; dirtied plates and mugs with only dregs of beer left inside them topped several of the tables, waiting to be cleared away.

Lawrence himself had supped at the long wooden bar which ran the length of the room. From this vantage point he watched as a young woman – clearly the daughter of the innkeeper and his wife, for she had her father's blue eyes and her mother's copper hair, though none of either's hearty girth – came quietly into the space and began to gather up the used dishes.

She kept her head down and eyes fixed on the floor as she murmured a startled and apologetic greeting. Clearly she had thought the room to be empty of patrons, and Lawrence's presence was as unexpected to her as hers was to him.

Lawrence mumbled his own excuses as the girl sidled past him. He kept his seat, all thoughts of bed forgotten, and watched as she moved about the room.

Quickly he realized that the young woman had an abnormality of some kind – her left arm was kept pressed against her stomach, held against her in a kind of sling tucked under a woolen shawl.

Of course, he thought, *of course there's something wrong with her.*

The bed was soft, the blankets warm, yet Lawrence could not sleep. When he closed his eyes, the young woman's face danced before him: kind, gentle eyes and soft lips.

More than once he found himself drifting into blissful dreams of burying his face in those long auburn tresses. And the way she had averted her eyes as she came near him, the way she had spoken to him with reverence and respect… the girl would be perfect, were it not for that arm.

Lawrence woke late the next morning, surprised he had slept at all, but determined in his mind to find out exactly what malady had befallen this otherwise perfect girl.

He found the innkeeper quietly polishing glasses behind the bar and, not one to beat about the push, came right out with it and asked the man what was wrong with his daughter.

The innkeeper told his guest a sad story. The young woman – Caroline – had, as a small child, fallen beneath the wheels of her father's wagon. The resulting damage to the girl's arm had caused the limb to lose all feeling and function, and eventually to be taken off completely by the surgeon in the nearest city.

The girl had worn several false arms over the years as she grew, new ones being whittled with each growth spurt in order to keep up.

For her twenty-first birthday, just a few months past, her father, still full of guilt over her injury, presented her with a gift of rare price: now that she had stopped growing, he had commissioned for her a new arm, one worthy of her.

An arm of solid gold.

Lawrence considered this. A woman with a missing arm was unthinkable. But a woman with an arm of solid gold… that changed things.

Aside from the strangeness of that one limb, the girl was beautiful, fit, quiet, and submissive. The perfect wife. The perfect wife with an arm worth more than his family's entire estate.

Lawrence spent a single week wooing the shy and disbelieving Caroline.

Seven days of courtship, then he dropped to one knee and asked for her hand (the non-golden one) in marriage. The betrothed partook of a quick and quiet ceremony in the town church, then Lawrence Hanover rode away toward his family home, with his new wife following close behind.

Although Caroline Hanover was equally beautiful to the most renowned maidens in the county, she was rarely seen outside the Hanover estate walls.

Lawrence was often seen about town on his own, doing business or passing a drowsy afternoon in the local pub, but Caroline was kept at home, her golden arm wrapped and held close against her, a secret only she and her new husband knew.

A sickness swept the area that summer, a miasma of infectious smog that seemed to rise from the verdant swamps and hover over the countryside. Countless people were taken ill; many died.

Among those affected were Lord and Lady Hanover, Lawrence's parents. For two weeks their home was filled with loud coughs and moist retchings.

The servants scurried about, full of whispered horror, and the doctor came and went, his face growing more haggard and less hopeful with each visit.

Lawrence's parents died on the same day, making him the new Lord Hanover.

His lovely wife became Lady Hanover just in time to be taken ill herself.

Lawrence saw the spots of blood on her fine white handkerchief. He gazed upon her sleeping form, taking in the dark crescents beneath her eyes, the paleness of her lips, the hint of gleaming gold that peeked out from the lacy sleeve of her nightgown.

He thought over the months since he had arrived home with his new bride in tow, thought long and hard about the life he had wished for so long to live and the life he had instead found himself in.

Lawrence Hanover discovered, when he looked honestly into the depths of his own soul, that he did not want a wife after all.

No doctor came to tend to the new Lady Hanover's illness. The servants were forbidden to enter that part of the house in which Caroline lay coughing and wheezing, twisted in her sweat-soaked bed sheets.

It took four days for her to die.

It took four hours for a grave to be dug, a plain wooden coffin knocked together, and for young, beautiful, tragic Caroline Hanover to be buried.

It took Lawrence most of the night to dig her back up.

Not all of her, of course.

He scraped away the dirt from the coffin, pried the lid open, and hastily unfastened the straps which held the heavy golden arm against the severed stump of his dead wife's arm.

The coffin lid was returned, the dirt shoveled back on top of it, and Lord Lawrence Hanover, dirty and sweating, crept back up to his bedroom with the golden arm tucked beneath his jacket.

He washed off as well as he could without calling for help, pulled on clean, dry undergarments, and crawled into bed to sleep away the coming day under the guise of grief.

Evening settled over the Hanover estate. The servants kept to themselves, turning in for the night as soon as their tasks were completed, leaving the master of the house to roam in quiet mourning.

Mourning, however, was the furthest thing from Lawrence's mind. He had not spared his beautiful young wife a second thought once he had the arm in his possession.

He pulled it from the bureau were he had stashed it upon waking at noon. The arm had a surprising weight to it; Lawrence wondered how Caroline had managed to walk around with it strapped to her shoulder.

His wife was dead. His parents were dead. The whole of the family estate was his to enjoy – or sell off – as he wished.

And the arm would fetch the loveliest price of all, if only he could manage to be patient. It wouldn't do to set off on an adventure just yet, and there was no way he could sell the arm in any of the nearest towns.

He would need to journey to one of the further cities, to a place where merchants had enough money to purchase his treasure.

And where he would not be recognized.

He had not murdered his wife, not exactly. But neither had he tried to save her.

The guilt was only the slightest ping against the edge of the happy fantasies he allowed himself to indulge in, fantasies of all the adventures he could take, paid for by that blessed golden arm.

Lawrence felt restless, stuffy inside the closed rooms of the house. He needed air, to stretch his legs. A walk around the grounds would do him good.

He made a circuit of the gardens, walking the carefully landscaped paths while dreaming of lusher, wilder places. Darkness fell around him; the sculptures took on strange new angles, the daytime hum faded to evening quiet.

Lawrence wiped away the sweat that beaded along his brow. He felt better now that he had expended a bit of energy, felt less like he was going to go crashing through walls or bouncing against the ceilings.

What he needed now was a cold drink and a good night's sleep.

He caught the movement just out of the corner of his eye. It was a slight thing, a wisp of light against the nighttime darkness. Lawrence stopped, one hand on the handle of the door that led back into the house.

He stood for a few moments, waiting, watching. He had just decided that it must have been a trick of the light – what little light there was – and turned to go inside when it came again.

A column of smoky light rose up from the ground at the edge of the woods, wavered a moment, then dissipated. As Lawrence watched in confusion, the mist rose again and again, each time a little denser, a little higher, a little steadier, as if gaining strength.

With a jolt, Lawrence realized where he was staring. A slight rise in the ground hid it from view, but the new Lord Hanover knew it was there.

The graveyard.

His hands pawed at the door, panic making him fumble for a moment before finally grasping the handle and yanking the door open. Lawrence tumbled into the house and slammed the door behind him, sliding the lock into place as quicky as he could.

Moments passed; nothing happened. No mist rose from beyond the small hill. No ghostly apparition appeared. Lawrence forced himself to take several shaking breaths. Now he really needed a drink.

He settled into the armchair near the window in the study, alternately sipping bourbon and peering out through the glass at the night beyond.

The liquor's warmth spread through him; his breathing slowed and his trembling hands stilled. As his mind settled into the calm familiarity of the bourbon's aftermath, he laughed at himself.

Still, he checked out the window one last time before he took himself – slowly, carefully, holding tight to the rail with one hand as he ascended the stairs – up to bed.

Lawrence slid the golden arm beneath his pillow and laid back against it. It was a strangely comforting feeling, as if Caroline herself were in bed next to him, with her arm cradling his head.

He lay in bed, his mind blessedly fuzzy around the edges, drifting in and out of conscious thought, blissful in his numbness.

Downstairs, a brief but powerful wind flung open the French doors in the library, and a strangely animate fog crept across the threshold.

Lawrence jerked awake. He didn't know if he'd been asleep for hours or minutes. His thoughts seemed sluggish; his body moved in slow-motion.

He lay in the darkness, in the stillness and the silence, fighting against the sleep which tried to pull him back into its depths, trying to discern what had woken him.

His bedroom door stood ajar. Clearly, he had been too drunk to bother closing it when he came in. He ran his hands over his body. Still fully dressed. Christ, he hadn't even taken his shoes off.

He struggled to keep his eyes open, struggled to keep his thoughts coherent and anchored in the moment. He glanced toward the window. Beyond, the night sky was purest black, dotted with silver stars.

A sound made his head jerk toward the door. What had it been? A voice? A whisper?

A strange, low light seemed to flood the hall beyond his room.

There, he heard it again. A woman's voice; quiet, soft, gentle, imploring.

He strained his ears to make out the words.

Where is my golden arm?

Lawrence gasped and sat up in bed, pulling the covers up around his chest like a frightened child.

The light came nearer, spreading along the fading wallpaper.

Rising. Up the stairs.

The voice sounded again.

Where is my golden arm?

Lawrence cowered, his back pressed against the headboard, watching in dreadful anticipation as the pale light grew stronger.

An ashen fog crept around the edge of the doorframe, rolling into the room and spreading along the floor, reaching out its long fingers toward the bed. From the head of the stairs the voice came again, louder.

Where is my golden arm?

Lawrence slid a hand beneath the pillow, his fingers closing around the cold, heavy limb. He pulled the arm out and cradled it against his chest, an ineffective talisman against the spirit he knew would soon appear in his doorway.

Mist filled the room. It reached the walls and rose upward, stretching across the ceiling only to drop heavy, damp tendrils downward like reaching vines.

Lawrence's eyes darted back and forth from the dripping fog to the ever-lightening doorway.

Light flickered across the wall beyond the door, a sickly candle-gutter against the darkness. A shadow stretched, grew taller, crept closer in disjointed motion.

Where is my golden arm?

The voice was soft, quiet, unmistakable.

Caroline. She was coming.

The room swirled with fog now, a maelstrom of malevolent mist, wrapping itself around the bed in which Lawrence sat, holding the arm close. The outside world seemed to not exist; Lawrence's whole mind was concentrated on this room, this moment, this anticipatory dread.

He watched in terror as the ghost appeared in the doorway, a gathering of smoke in the shape of his wife. Her body seemed lopsided, off-kilter; Lawrence could not take his eyes away from her left side, where the absence of an arm created a blank darkness, an uncanny emptiness.

The specter glided toward him, the fog which covered the floor rolling back before her. Lawrence could not move. He stared up into Caroline's face as a cold blue flame flared to life in her eyes.

She reached the bed; the mist followed her, stretching out from her insubstantial skirts to flood the bed top. Lawrence felt himself a small island in an ever-encroaching ocean of fog.

Caroline's form leaned toward him. Her mouth opened; the words which echoed out from the hollow beyond were both quiet and powerful.

Where is my golden arm?

Those blue-flamed eyes dropped from Lawrence's face to the thing he held in his arms.

Caroline's voice was stronger now.

Give me my golden arm!

Lawrence trembled as the spirit reached toward him. The pale, ghostly fingers curled around the golden arm.

Lawrence's voice came out as barely more than a breath.

"Take it!"

Paralyzing cold gripped his heart as the ghost of his wife rushed toward him and tore the arm from his grasp.

Lawrence's mouth opened and closed; there seemed to be no air in the room for him to pull into his lungs.

Caroline's form faded; it dissipated into the fog, then the fog itself retreated from the bed, from the room, from the house.

The next morning, the maid who came to stoke the fire in young Lord Hanover's bedroom began to scream.

The other servants came rushing in; the plump housekeeper took the maid into her arms and turned her away from the gruesome sight.

Lawrence Hanover's corpse sat against the pillows, under the blankets yet fully clothed, his face distorted in a rictus of fear and his arms seeming to grasp something against his chest, the muscles frozen in a bizarre grip on empty air.

In a bustling inn two days' ride from the Hanover estate, a burly innkeeper named Burris woke to his wife's piercing shriek.

He came up out of bed with fists swinging and a string of profanities ready to issue forth, but the words never left his mouth; dumbfounded silence overtook the room as he saw that thing to which his wife pointed.

There, in place of honor between two tall candlesticks on the fireplace mantel, lay their daughter's golden arm.

The Cold Man

Where do the scary things come from?

The world is full of stories of bogeymen and bugbears, ghouls and haunts and all manner of nighttime creatures. The storytellers make up the plot, the background, the modus operandi, *but what really brings the creatures to life? What takes them from the realm of story and lets them slither-sneak, hither-creep out into that realm we call the real world?*

It is belief, dear readers.

Imagination creates the monsters; belief makes them real.

And no belief is more strong, more unshakable, more horribly innocent than that of a child.

This is the story of how a little boy brought a bogeyman into the world.

Eleven years separated Rachel Carson from her younger brother, Danny, but the two were thick as thieves, best buddies. Danny looked up to Rachel with all the admiration a five-year-old could muster, and

Rachel looked back down to him with a selfless love uncommon in a sixteen-year-old girl.

It was October, and, as Ray Bradbury said, October is a rare month for boys. It was a rare month indeed for a little boy like Danny, who loved spooky stories.

He had taught himself to read over the last few months and had devoured every children's Halloween book he could get his hands on, all the ones passed down to him from his three older siblings and all the ones his mother could find to check out from the library.

It was a sunny October afternoon, and Danny and Rachel sat side by side on the living room couch, with the windows open behind them to let in the fresh autumn air.

Danny had a pile of picture books stacked next to him and held them up one by one to show his sister, telling her what each one was about. Rachel smiled and nodded in all the right places, attentive to her little brother's words and amused by his excitement.

She was caught off guard a little, however, when he asked the question, "Do you know any scary stories, Rachel?"

Rachel thought quickly, frantically, searching her brain for a story.

Her mind went blank. She couldn't remember a single one.

Danny's little face looked up at her, excited, expectant. She couldn't let him down. She cast about for an idea, letting her gaze drift out the open window to the street beyond. The giant cottonwood out front had covered the yard with a blanket of golden leaves.

Up and down the street, porches were decorated with pumpkins waiting to be carved. Fake spiderwebs stretched from bare tree limbs and Styrofoam tombstones grew like weeds from otherwise respectable lawns.

Every house on the street was decorated in some way, big or small.

Every house except one.

The occupant of the house directly across the street had been the subject of imaginative debate among the three older Carson children for some time.

There were a few facts they had determined about this elusive individual. He was a single man. No one else ever entered or exited the house.

He had no running water; the place where his water meter should have been stood empty.

He likely slept all day, with blackout shades over all the windows and no sign of life before five o'clock in the afternoon.

He left the house almost every evening around seven, loading multiple empty water jugs into his car and returning half an hour later with full jugs and wet hair; the siblings surmised that he went somewhere during that half hour to take a shower and refill his water supply for the day.

He left the house again around nine o'clock most nights, dressed entirely in black, with a guitar case in hand, and did not return again until the wee hours of the morning.

It made logical sense that the man was a musician, probably playing back-up at some club or another, making barely enough money to pay the rent and certainly not enough to pay the water bill.

Logical stories being generally boring, the Carson teenagers had passed a lazy afternoon or two dreaming up far more interesting backgrounds for the neighbor they called the Cube Man, due to the kind of car he drove.

That he was a creature of the night was unquestionable, but whether vampire, demon, ghost, or serial killer was the question that kept the conversation going.

Rachel pulled upon bits of these conversations now as she created a story for little Danny.

"You see that house across the street there, the one that looks like nobody lives in it?"

Danny sat up on his knees, his arms on the windowsill, looking at the house Rachel pointed to. He nodded.

"Well, the man that lives there is really creepy. He only comes out at night."

Danny's eyes grew large and round as he looked back and forth from his sister to the house across the street.

Rachel settled into the story, the words coming out of her mouth as quickly as her brain came up with the ideas.

"Do you see the creatures on the roof?"

Danny's eyes shot to the house, eyes scanning. He looked at Rachel as if he wasn't quite sure whether to believe her or not.

"No? Well, most people can't see them. Only a special few can. I can see them. Should I tell you what they look like?"

Danny paused, uncertain for a moment, before nodding.

"They look like aliens, or like giant buggy things. All skin and scales and long legs like spiders. There's two of them on the roof. There's only room for two. That's how big they are. Two giant, spider-alien creatures."

"What are they doing there?" Danny's voice was barely more than a whisper.

"Oh, right now they're just sitting there. They only move when the man who lives there tells them to, and so they sleep during the day just like he does. But when night comes, and the man wakes up, he sends them out.

"They're Dream-Suckers. They scuttle onto the roofs of houses where everyone is asleep, and they reach their long skinny legs down into the windows, and they stick themselves to people's heads and suck out their dreams."

Danny dropped away from the window, pulling his knees to his chest and wrapping his arms around them. He didn't want to look at the house across the street anymore.

Rachel went on.

"And then, when they're full of dreams, they come back to their house, across the street. They empty out all the dreams into giant barrels in the basement of the house, and the man uses them to make himself stronger. He eats the dreams like you eat pizza. And then, when enough nights have passed, and he's eaten enough dreams to be strong again, the man goes out."

"What does he do?" Danny's voice shook just a little.

"He sneaks into the bedrooms of little boys."

"And then what?" Now his voice shook a lot.

"He creeps right up to their beds… and he looks for any little hands or feet sticking out from under the blankets, and then he reaches out and…"

"And what?" Danny hid his face in his arms, only his blue eyes peeking up at his sister as he spoke.

"And he… touches them with his long, cold fingers!"

Danny waited a moment, waited for more, waited for something truly horrible.

Rachel had run out of ideas.

"That's it. He just touches you with his cold hands. That's what he's called. The Cold Man. He makes you cold. So if you wake up in the middle of the night and your arm or leg is out from under the covers and it's cold, it's because the Cold Man has just been there, touching you with his icy fingers."

Danny's face as he looked up at her was full of derision. "That's all? He just touches you and makes you cold?"

Rachel reached out and mussed the blonde curls of Danny's hair. "That's it, kiddo. That's what he does. He's the Cold Man."

She stretched her fingers out in front of her and wiggled them menacingly. Danny rolled his eyes and laughed.

And that was that.

Except that it wasn't.

That night, as Danny lay in bed, he thought about the story his sister had told him. It had seemed dumb at first – who would ever be scared of someone just because they made you cold?

But as he stared at his nightlight and listened to the muffled sounds and voices of his parents and older siblings as they moved around the house, he began to feel just the tiniest bit frightened.

He thought about the man across the street and the Dream-Suckers on the roof. He wondered if any of Rachel's story was true. It *was* true that the man only came out at night, even Danny knew that. But the rest of the story was just made-up.

Wasn't it?

Danny burrowed down inside his covers, just to be safe, just to be sure, just in case. He wrapped the blankets tightly around himself, tucking the ends beneath him, so that he looked like a mummy as he lay in bed, with his arms and legs held in close and only his eyes and nose sticking out.

He fell into an uneasy sleep.

He dreamed of giant spider-like creatures that crawled and ran across the rooftops.

In the darkness of a world beyond our own, something stirred. A vague shape began to take form. It floated, weightless, waiting.

Danny woke the next morning drenched in sweat and had to work to extricate himself from his blanket cocoon.

By breakfast-time he had forgotten the dreams.

But he hadn't forgotten the Cold Man, and Rachel found him later that afternoon, sitting on the front steps, chin in hand, staring at the house across the street, deep in thought. Rachel sat down next to him, nudged him with her elbow.

"Whatcha doin', kiddo?"

Danny looked up at her and sighed. "Nothing."

Rachel, being a perceptive older sister, knew that *nothing* was definitely *something*.

"Come on, Danny. Tell me what's on your mind."

Danny shrugged and went back to staring at the house across the street. Rachel followed his line of sight and had to force herself to keep a straight face as she spoke.

"Thinking about the Cold Man, huh?"

Danny looked up at her so quickly that she jerked back from him. He was troubled by the name, by the story, she could tell.

"Oh, Danny," she said, and she wrapped an arm around him and pulled him into a hug. "Don't worry about it, kid. It's just a story I made up. It's not real at all."

"Are you sure?" Danny asked, and she assured him that there was absolutely nothing to be afraid of.

And yet.

That night Danny tossed and turned for hours without falling asleep. Every time he closed his eyes he pictured a man, with dark clothes and pale skin, eyes like black holes in a long face, with fingers much too long, that reached out toward him in the darkness of his bedroom.

He tried wrapping himself up in the blankets again but the day had been unseasonably warm and he began sweating within minutes. The sweating made him itchy and before long he had stuck a leg out from the blankets, letting it jut out over the edge of the bed. It took him a moment to realize his mistake. He jerked the leg back, covering it carefully up again with the blanket.

Danny dozed, his mind alive with the vision it had conjured, the vision of the Cold Man.

The form which floated in the nothingness took on definition. It formed itself into the shape of a man. Dark spots bloomed where eyes should be, dark ink ran along arms and legs until something like clothing appeared. Fingers elongated, the skin beneath the fingernails an icy blue. The thing leaned forward, listening, waiting.

Finally, Danny got out of bed and turned his bedroom light on. The clock on his bookshelf said 12:35 in blazing red numbers. He hadn't learned how to read the big round clocks yet.

With the light on, he felt a little safer, and before long his eyes closed and he drifted off to sleep.

The thing about Oklahoma weather is that it changes rapidly. The unseasonably warm day had indeed turned into an unseasonably warm night, but now that unseasonable warmth was fleeing before a long line of autumn storms.

At 1:30, the first roll of thunder rumbled through the air.

By 2:00, the wind gusts had reached seventy miles an hour and the lightning shot in jagged bolts from sky to ground.

At 2:47 exactly, the power went out.

Danny's comforting light went dark.

With the squall line came plummeting temperatures. An eighty-degree day had become a seventy-degree evening which quickly became a forty-degree night.

With the power out, the heater did not kick in as the thermostat plunged below the programmed threshold.

The house, without electricity to power the lights, was dark.

The house, without electricity to power the various machines which hummed and gurgled through the night, was quiet.

The house, without electricity to power the heater, was cold.

Danny awoke with a vague feeling of wrongness.

He could hear his own breathing, his own heartbeat thumping in his ears.

The thing crept from the darkness of its creation.

Danny pulled the blankets up around his face. His eyes, pale orbs shining in the darkness, looked from one corner of the room to another.

There, just beside the window. Danny swore he saw movement.

The thing took a step forward.

Danny ducked his head under the covers.

The air turned frigid as the Cold Man crept, hunched, along the floor of the child's room.

Danny trembled beneath his blankets. He shook his head to deny the thought that raced through his mind. *It's just a story Rachel made up. It's just pretend. There's nothing there. Don't be a baby. Be brave. It's just a story.*

Danny let one toe creep cautiously out from under his quilt.

He slid his foot out, paused.

The room was cold, and he shivered. He let his ankle slide out, his shin. His leg was dangling now over the side of the bed. *For a count of ten,* he told himself, *then I'll know it's safe, that it was just a story.*

One.

Two.

The thing looked at the boy in the bed.

Three.

Four.

It looked at the bare little foot, stretched out like a perfect offering.

Five.

Six.

The Cold Man reached out his long, pale hands, fingers like spider's legs.

Seven.

Eight.

It wrapped its cold fingers around the small ankle.

Danny felt the chill, a ring of ice encircling his leg, a cold that penetrated so deeply it hurt. For one shocked moment he held perfectly still, perfectly silent, his mind refusing to believe the messages his frosty skin was sending.

And then he screamed.

He screamed and he screamed and he screamed.

His parents came running. His siblings came running.

With flashlights and lighted candles, they pushed their way into his room. His mother pulled the blankets back from Danny's head and held him close against her.

"What's wrong, baby?" she asked, running her hands along his head, his neck, his shoulders. "Are you hurt somewhere?"

Danny's terrified eyes lifted and scanned the people crowded around him.

He settled his gaze on Rachel's face, and a sinking feeling of guilt and shame dropped into her gut as he whispered, "It was the Cold Man."

Behind the gathered family, beyond that veil which separates the light from the darkness, a pale figure with black eyes and skin like snow shivered with power
and faded into the night.

Rachel Carson spent the next two months trying to convince her little brother that the Cold Man was not real, that she had made him up on the spot, off the top of her head, that he was absolutely not something to worry about.

Just before Christmas, the man who lived in the house across the street moved out, leaving nothing behind but an overgrown lawn and a traumatized little boy.

Through the rest of his childhood, Danny Carson, while laughing off the idea of the Cold Man and blustering on bravely about what a silly thing it was to be afraid of someone whose worst threat was that they made you cold, would still, each night, sleep in a room with the lights dimmed but not turned out, with every part of his body cocooned in layers of blankets, no matter how much he sweated inside them.

Just to be sure.

Just to be safe.
Just in case.

Somewhere else in the world, or perhaps multiple somewheres, far away or just a block over, an idea, fully formed, popped into the mind of another person, another child or another adult, another imagination: the image of a man with pale skin and dark eyes and fingers like ice.

The idea of him was out there, the story begun. In the darkness of the void the Cold Man stepped forth, ready for whatever new changes or nuances might be assigned to him as the story changed and morphed and grew and took on new characteristics.

The Cold Man smiled a frozen smile and cracked his long, frozen fingers and simply waited to be called.

BENEATH THE BED

Bill Coffey was getting up there in years; he couldn't remember the exact number anymore, but he'd been around long enough to know the scent on the air that meant rain was coming, to recognize the signs of a late frost determined to kill his spring crops, and to predict the harshness of the coming winter by the shapes hidden in the persimmons and the stripes on the wooly bear caterpillars.

This year, the persimmons had shown the shape of a sharp knife, a sign that the approaching winter would be harshly cold with biting winds. The woolly bears had agreed, showing wide black stripes and only the thinnest band of rusty brown in between. Winter was going to be long and cold.

Which wasn't really any surprise at all.

Bill's sons didn't care much for farm work now that they were grown, but they loved their old dad enough to come and help at harvest time just the same. Thanks to their younger, stronger bodies, all the crops had been brought in, and just in time. The wheat and the corn and the sorghum, all were cut and flailed and sifted, stored away in enormous bins out in the barn, dry and warm for the coming season.

Of course, Bill's wife, Alice, had been hard at work in her own way. While Bill and the boys were in charge of the fields and the grains, Alice had spent the last fifty-some-odd years of her life tending her vegetable garden and her chickens.

For the past eight weeks, Alice had been having a harvest of her own. Tomatoes cooked and canned as tomato sauce and soup, cucumbers made into pickles, peppers chopped and boiled and sealed into jars of brine, carrots and potatoes and onions by the crate-full stored in the cool, dry root cellar.

Yes, as the late-autumn sun sank over the western hills that evening and Bill and Alice Coffey sat in their rocking chairs on the porch of their old farmhouse, a feeling of peaceful contentment was in the air. Another year of farming, of living, done. Another winter's worth of food stored safely away.

A match flared in the darkness as Bill lit up. Alice watched him stand and walk to the edge of the porch, a dark silhouette against an indigo sky.

Bill stood for a moment, puffing on his pipe, then he went down the front steps and stood for a bit out in the front yard.

"A good thing I tightened up your hen house yesterday," he said, not bothering to turn his head toward his wife.

"Oh?" she said, "You feel weather comin' on?"

Bill stood for a minute longer before turning and walking back up the steps. "It's comin'," he said. "And it's comin' fast."

Bill was right; he always was. He had grown up on this land, he knew every curve of every hill, every secret trail through the woods, every nuance of the air and sky that signaled a change in the weather.

Within the hour, rain began to fall, tiny pinpricks of water at first that changed quickly to a downpour of fat, heavy drops. Alice shivered as she stood to go inside. The temperature was dropping fast. Overnight it would surely drop below freezing.

Bill stoked up a pleasant fire in the old stone fireplace. Alice lit a couple of the hurricane lamps she'd inherited, along with the house, from Bill's mother.

They settled in, he with the newspaper and she with a book, each next to their own lamp, to read for as long as their tired eyes would let them.

The rain pounded steadily on the old metal roof. A wind from the north hurled drops against the windows. Deep growls of thunder boomed far off in the distance. Alice looked up, startled, at a sudden crash from the back of the house.

Bill stood and put a reassuring hand on her shoulder. "Probably just the back door banging in the wind. Not sure I latched it proper last time I came in."

Alice nodded and dropped her eyes back to her book but raised them again as soon as Bill's back was turned, watching him cross the wide front room and go through the door in the back.

She listened to the heavy clump of his old work boots as he walked across their bedroom to the back door. She heard the door close firmly, and the latch click into place.

Bill returned to the front room and smiled. "Not a thing to worry about, dear. Just an old man who forgets to close doors properly and a clever wind intent on tattling on him."

Alice smiled and went back to her book.

When the old clock on the mantel chimed nine times, Bill stood and stretched and announced that he was going to bed.

Alice lifted her face for a quick kiss. "I'll be in shortly," she said, and Bill went into the back room, leaving her alone with the dying fire.

Alice read until the words began to blur on the page. In the bedroom, Bill's steady snores, louder even than the thunder, signaled that he was already sound asleep.

Outside, the storm continued. The sound of sharper hits upon the window glass told Alice that the rain was slowly turning over to sleet.

It would be a frozen world when they woke up the next morning, she was sure of it.

Alice yawned as she turned out the lamps and banked the last embers of the fire to keep them smoldering until sunrise. She took a moment to look out the window, where sheets of water obscured the darkened land beyond. She checked that the front door was latched, remembering that Bill had latched the back one earlier after the wind banged it open and not wishing for a repeat of that startling sound.

Alice went into the bedroom and stripped off her daytime clothes before slipping into her comfortable old flannel nightgown.

She left on her long underwear and a pair of thick woolen socks beneath it. As she climbed into bed, she stepped in a small spot of icy-cold water that made her suck in a hissing breath.

Some rain must have blown in when the door was open, she thought as she hoisted herself up into the high bed and pulled the heavy blankets up around her face.

The warmth of the bed and her husband's trapped body heat spread slowly through her old bones, and her body relaxed.

Bill's snores continued; she had grown so used to them over the years that she hardly noticed them anymore.

Alice was just on the edge of sleep when she felt the mattress shift. Her eyes opened and she grunted a bit. Bill must have been dreaming, moving about in his sleep, disturbing her.

Outside a jagged line of lightning lit the world. Sleet tapped on the window. Alice snuggled deeper down into her pillow. Her eyes blinked a few times, struggling to stay open.

Another flash of lightning lit the room, and something caught Alice's attention, though she couldn't quite pinpoint what it was.

Her eyes opened wider now, brows furrowed.

In that momentary flash of light, something had been wrong. But what was it?

Alice waited. Moments later, another flash, and she saw them: small puddles of water all across the bedroom floor.

They led from the bed to the back door.

Or was it from the door to the bed?

Alice turned this over in her half-asleep mind.

They looked like footsteps. Like the mess Bill made when he came clomping in from the fields on a rainy day, dripping water and mud in his wake.

But Bill hadn't been outside in the rain. They'd both been safely ensconced in the house before it started. He had gone to close the door when it blew open, but he hadn't gone outside then, had he?

Surely, even if he had stepped out on the small back stoop for a moment, he wouldn't have stood there in the rain long enough to make watery footprints when he came back inside.

An uneasiness settled in Alice's gut. She let her eyes roam over the darkness of their bedroom. The room, like everything else in their lives, was sparse.

The bed stood against one wall, a small chest with a water pitcher against another, a line of hooks on which they hung their clothes against a third wall, and the door to the front room stood on the fourth. There was nowhere for a person to hide. Nowhere except…

The mattress shifted once more beneath Alice, and the realization hit her with complete clarity and utter dread.

Someone was under the bed.

Slowly, she turned in the bed. The shifting beneath her became more pronounced, and she could swear she felt the bony point of an elbow through the mattress. Finally, she turned enough to face Bill. He continued snoring, oblivious to the horrific situation Alice now found herself in.

"Bill," she whispered, but he did not give the slightest indication that he had heard her.

"Bill!" A little louder this time.

Bill did not stir, but from beneath the bed came a hard shove that nearly rolled her right over the edge. Alice gasped and threw her arms out to steady herself.

She didn't dare to speak again, but laid there in the darkness, her heart pounding, the comforting warmth that had settled over her moments earlier now gone, replaced with icy streams of fear.

Another shove from underneath. Alice held on to the headboard. Bill grunted and for a brief shining moment Alice thought he would wake up, but he sucked in a sharp snort and resumed snoring.

Alice cursed under her breath.

"Bill!" Her voice was louder this time, and the jolt from below was stronger. Alice was raised a few inches off the mattress, hands scrabbling against the wall as she lost her grip on the headboard.

Bill's eyes opened. Alice's face was turned toward him, her own eyes huge and filled with fear. Bill's brow creased, and he opened his mouth to speak but Alice shook her head frantically.

"Shhh," she whispered, and not daring to speak aloud, she mouthed the next words: *keep snoring.*

Bill looked at her like she had lost her mind. Frustrated, she kept her eyes locked on his as her fingers stretched up, seeking the item they had brushed against briefly after that last hard shove, seeking the thing which hung on the wall just above the bed.

The rain continued to pound steadily on the roof. From beneath the bed came the distinct knocking sounds of someone moving around in a cramped space, elbows against wood as whoever was hiding down there turned themself over and made ready to slide out.

"Bill." Alice's breath was barely audible, but Bill was wide awake now and listening.

"There's someone under the bed."

Alice pointed down with her left hand as her right hand slid further up the wall.

"Keep snoring."

Bill stared at her for a moment before he realized what she was doing. Nodding slightly, he sucked in a loud snorting breath. Alice nodded back and rolled her hand to indicate that he should continue.

Bill let out one measured, grunting snore after another as Alice's hand found what it sought: the hunting rifle that Bill had inherited from his father.

The one he had sat down every Saturday night for fifty years to clean and oil and reload, just in case. The one that had only been used twice in all the time they'd been married, to shoot the mangy wolves that sometimes came too close to the henhouse.

Alice lifted the gun down carefully, quietly, any small noises she made covered by the loud rattle of Bill's snores.

She laid the gun gently between them on the bed, then pushed herself up against the pillows with agonizing slowness.

She shifted to the side, as far as she could without falling off the bed.

She picked up the gun again, burying the muzzle far down into the feather-filled mattress until she felt it strain against the bottom layer of ticking.

Alice raised her eyes to meet Bill's, wrapped her finger firmly around the trigger, and mouthed the words: *one…two…three.*

Everything happened at once.

The sound of the shot exploded through the room.

A strangled shout from beneath the bed told Alice she'd found her mark.

The scents of gunpowder and blood mixed in the air.

The brightest bolt of lightning yet lit the sight of an arm flung outward along the floor, and, already, the edge of a quickly expanding pool of crimson blood.

Bill climbed out of bed and pulled Alice off behind him, on his side, away from the arm and the blood and whoever they both belonged to. He took the gun from his wife's trembling hands and made his way cautiously around the bed.

"Light, please, Alice," he said, and Alice hurried back into the front room to fetch a lamp.

By the glow of the small flame, the farmer and his wife stood looking at the arm, at the fingers which twitched slowly, at the spreading stain on the wooden boards.

"Take this." Bill handed the gun back to his wife. "And keep it trained, just in case."

Alice nodded, raising the rifle to her shoulder and pointing it toward the bed.

Bill approached cautiously, reaching down and grasping the bloody hand. He pulled. An awful moan escaped the man that slid slowly from under the bed, a sound of pain and fear like a dying animal.

The bullet had gone straight through the feather mattress and directly into the center of the man's bare chest. Blood pumped furiously, welling up and then overflowing, streaming down his ribs to the floor.

Alice barely recognized the sound at first. The pounding on the front door seemed to mirror exactly the pounding of her own heart.

Bill put a calming hand on her arm. "Stay here, keep that gun up." Alice's head dipped slightly in agreement.

Bill went through to the front room. Alice's eyes stayed fixed on the man who lay motionless on her bedroom floor as she listened to the commotion behind her.

There was the creak of the door opening, men's voices, quiet at first but growing louder, the stomping of many boots. She heard the words but only half processed them as the shock set in.

"... sheriff … murder … cover of the storm … escaped … dangerous …"

Alice flinched as a hand touched her shoulder.

"Shh, Alice, it's just me."

Bill's voice was quiet. He took the gun from her and wrapped an arm around her shoulder, pulling her close against him.

In the dim light she recognized Sheriff Jameson and a couple of the other men from town.

Alice was suddenly aware that she was standing in her nightgown, and she scurried back to stand behind her husband as the lawmen approached the body.

Sheriff Jameson knelt down, careful to avoid the blood, and pressed his fingers to the man's neck.

"Dead as a doornail," he said.

He straightened up. "Dan, Benjamin, ride back to town and get the wagon. Bill, Alice, we'll get this cleaned up quick as we can. It's a miracle you two managed this. This fellow – George Bryson – was being held over in Cliffton on four counts of murder.

"Seems he snuck into people's houses and hid beneath their beds till they were asleep, then knocked them onto the floor and stabbed them before they even had a chance to wake up.

"Y'all are lucky to be alive."

Bill snorted.

"Luck ain't got nothing to do with it, Sheriff. Unless it's the luck I happened into when I married this here fine woman."

Alice peeked out from behind her husband, brushing long gray strands of hair away from her face, and smiled.

The Creature that Drains the Blood from the Sheep

Mrs. Lopez was one of those teachers that all the kids loved. She taught four different classes each day – two periods of Musical Theory and one each of Musical Composition and Choir – and within the first two weeks of school she knew every student's name.

She knew about their home lives; she knew about their friends. She knew where they struggled and where they excelled.

She knew which ones liked to work in groups and which ones liked to go it alone, which ones had the self-confidence to belt out a solo and which ones needed a little encouragement.

Mrs. Lopez was still relatively young herself, and this helped her relate to the trials and tribulations that befall all adolescents at one time or another.

At twenty-eight, Nina Lopez could have easily passed as one of the high school students who filled her classroom, if it weren't for one thing: Nina Lopez's long, silky hair was pure white.

There was some speculation among her students as to the cause of this curiosity. Some thought she bleached it, some that she had been born that way.

A few suggested it might be a wig. One student brought in their older brother's yearbook from five years earlier, the first year Nina Lopez – then Nina Cardoza – had come to teach at East Creek High School.

Her hair in her staff photo had been a glossy black.

In her photo the very next year it had been white.

As the school year came to an end, one student – Brian Graff by name – worked up the courage to ask Mrs. Lopez outright. The last choir concert had been the week before; all there was left to do for the remaining minutes of the year was to lounge around and pass the time until the bell rang.

Mrs. Lopez was cleaning out her desk drawers while the students talked in small groups when Brian said her name.

"Mrs. Lopez?"

The teacher looked up, expecting to be asked for something trivial, a bathroom pass perhaps.

"Mrs. Lopez," Brian repeated, "what made your hair turn white like that?"

Nina Lopez was caught so off-guard by this question that she merely blinked in Brian's direction for a moment.

A swelling chorus of interest and support for this question arose from the other students. Mrs. Lopez swallowed, hard. She took a moment to consider the question.

"If I told you, you might not believe me," she said finally, and the class let out a collective groan.

"Come on, Mrs. Lopez. We'll believe you," Brian said, giving her his best puppy-dog eyes.

Mrs. Lopez looked around at the twenty-four faces that stared back at her expectantly. She closed the drawer she had just been sorting through and folded her hands on the desk in front of her.

"Alright," she said, and the class seemed to lean toward her in one fluid motion. "If you really want to know – oh, God, I hope I don't get in trouble for telling you this – here's the story of how my hair turned white..."

New Mexico, four years earlier

Nina Cardoza did not so much gaze out the window as stare fiercely. She was excited to see the ranch, excited to finally meet the family of her soon-to-be-husband.

Theirs had been a whirlwind romance, two months of intense and passionate dates before he dropped to one knee and popped the question. Of course, she'd said yes, and, in keeping with the pace they'd already established, the wedding date was set for three weeks later, to take place on Ben's family ranch in New Mexico.

Ben had assured her that his parents would love her and welcome her into the family with open arms. Nina had been uncertain.

Then Ben had begun to describe his family's ranch, all wide-open spaces, tufts of scrub grass, jagged mountains in the distance, purple sunsets. Nina's imagination had taken hold of his descriptions and run with them, her excitement at seeing this beautiful place replacing her trepidation about meeting Ben's family.

They had driven there, all the way from Sand Springs, across the entire state of Oklahoma, then the Texas panhandle, into New Mexico and almost to the Arizona border, to the Lopez Ranch.

They were almost there, Ben told her. Nina hoped so. They'd been driving for two days–eight hundred miles of flat, dry, brown land as far as the eye could see. Her eyes yearned for a break in the monotony, some color, some sign of life.

"Look, baby, up ahead."

Ben pointed with one hand and held the steering wheel loosely with the other.

Nina followed the direction of his finger. Ahead of them, in the distance, a line of gray-blue mountains ranged across the landscape. If she squinted, she could just make out the glistening white of their snow-capped tops.

"Almost there, baby, almost there," Ben reassured her, his pointing hand dropping to rest on her knee.

She gave him a small smile and then leaned forward, arms against the dashboard, eyes trained on the mountains ahead.

For a while it seemed as if they weren't getting any closer to the mountains at all. The road went on, a nearly-straight scar through the desert, and they followed it, the distant range remaining disconcertingly far away until suddenly it began to grow in Nina's vision.

Her eyes lifted up, up, and up as she tried to take in the vastness of it all.

The mountains loomed before them, and Nina could not shake the feeling that those massive rocks marked the end of the world somehow; she felt as though, if one were brave enough to scale the heights and look down over the other side, all one would see would be a vast dark emptiness beyond.

Ben pulled her from these troubling thoughts by squeezing her knee and telling her, once more, to look where he pointed.

Up ahead, in one mile or perhaps two, she saw a turnoff: the dusty road they were on birthing another, even dustier one heading south. Ben turned the car off onto this side road, and in no time at all they were driving through a huge metal gate over which arched a rust-flecked sign reading "Lopez."

Alongside the road there now ran miles of fencing, worn wooden posts strung with tight barbed wire. Far in the distance, Nina could see small specks of white and gray which she assumed must be sheep. Before long, a building appeared ahead of them, starting as a vague outline and growing more detailed as they drew closer.

Nina soon saw that it was not a single building, but a group of them. A large, low house sat at the end of the road, but behind it and stretching out in both directions were a number of other structures:

barns, tool sheds, shacks whose purpose Nina could not even begin to guess at.

Ben's hand squeezed Nina's knee again. "We're here!" he said, his face lighting up with a smile that Nina could not help but share.

He was cute, a little boy returned home, and she saw in him then a glimpse of the child that he once was.

They had barely stepped out of the car when the front door of the house opened and a woman came rushing out. She was short and plump, with dark hair pulled back in a braid which was then wound up into a bun.

"Benjamin!" she cried, and threw her arms around her son.

Nina stood awkwardly to the side until Ben introduced her. Nina had a moment of doubt, of fear, certain that Ben's mother would hate her on sight, but Regina Lopez gave her a warm smile and hugged her almost as fiercely as she had hugged Ben.

Regina ushered Nina inside, leaving Ben to carry in their luggage. A large kitchen stretched across the back of the house; three sets of double doors opened to the patio area beyond.

At the counter stood a girl perhaps a few years younger than Nina, her hands dusted with yellow flour as she rolled out tortillas.

Regina introduced her as Ben's little sister, Sofia.

Nina smiled and stretched out her arm for a handshake. Sofia arched an eyebrow and held out her own flour-covered hand. For a moment the two young women stood looking at each other, hands outstretched but not touching, then they both laughed.

Ben came in, arms full of bags, and dropped them on the floor.

"Give me just a minute," he gasped, "and I'll carry these up to my room."

The women rolled their eyes at his dramatic wheezing.

"You'll do no such thing," Regina said, and Ben looked at her for a moment in confusion.

Then understanding lit his face and he sighed.

"Mama, surely you aren't serious."

Regina Lopez put her hands on her hips and stared up into her son's face.

"I don't know what kind of dirty sinful things you've been doing out in Oklahoma, but you will not sleep together in *this* house until you are married!"

Ben met Nina's eyes over the top of his mother's head and he shrugged. Regina turned to Nina.

"Nina, *mija*, I have the cot on the porch all made up for you."

A cot on a porch did not sound to Nina like an ideal place to sleep, but eager to stay in her future mother-in-law's good graces, she smiled and said, "Thank you."

Ben sorted Nina's bags from his own and gestured for her to follow him. They went through a door off the side of the kitchen, through a short hallway, and then out onto a small porch.

The floor was red tile, the wooden framing painted a bright turquoise. Wire screens stretched all the way around, keeping out mosquitoes and other insects.

A door was set into the far wall, with steps leading out into the pasture beyond. In one corner a camp bed was made up with fluffy pillows and thin summer blankets.

Ben set Nina's luggage at the foot of the bed and looked around, rubbing the back of his neck.

"Honestly," he said, "you've probably got the best room in the house."

When Nina looked at him doubtfully, he went on.

"This time of year, the coolest place to sleep is outside. Here on the porch you'll at least get what little breeze comes through. You'll be sleeping like a princess while the rest of us are roasting alive upstairs."

Nina had a feeling he was just trying to make her feel better, but she loved him for it and let herself be folded into his arms.

"Just think," he said, kissing the top of her head, "tomorrow we'll be married."

Dinner that night was a grand affair, and Nina got the feeling that it was only slightly more grand that a normal dinner must be in the Lopez household. The kitchen was swelteringly hot by the end of the day, so they all ate outside on the patio, around an old square table.

Ben and Nina sat on one side, Ben's parents on another, Sofia had one side to herself, and the last side was taken by Ben's grandparents, who Nina had been instructed to call Abuela and Abuelo.

Food was in abundance, all kinds of delicious and spicy dishes that Nina had never seen or heard of before.

Conversation centered mostly around the wedding that would take place the following day. A simple ceremony would be held at the small chapel in town, then a larger reception back at the ranch.

All of Ben's extended family would be there, and from what Nina understood, the extended family was indeed extensive.

Regina, Sofia, and Abuela went on and on about all the preparations they had been making, the huge stores of food they had been preparing for the past week.

Nina kept fairly quiet, listening to the chatter, smiling and nodding in all the right places. Her belly was full, and after a long two days of driving she really wanted nothing more than to have a little time to herself and get some sleep. She could just see the corner of the sleeping porch from where she sat, and she hoped the bed would be comfortable; at this point, however, she figured she probably could have slept soundly enough on top of a bag of rocks.

A man's voice brought her back from her drowsy thoughts. Ben's father, Leo, was speaking.

Other than a mumbled "hello" earlier, this was the first time Nina had heard his voice. He spoke quietly, his words barely discernible over the sound of the crickets and tree frogs. Nina caught enough of his speech to trouble her, however, words like *dead, blood, sheep, monster.*

Regina gave Nina a sharp glance before standing abruptly. "That's enough of that. Sofia, help me clear the table. Ben, why don't you help Nina get settled on the porch? Then early to bed, everyone. We have a busy day tomorrow."

With a determined step and a look in her eye that brooked no argument, she began circling the table, picking up dishes.

Nina was certainly glad to slip into her nightgown, glad of the chance to relax, but she was curious about Leo's words.

When she returned from the bathroom in her gown and robe, Ben was waiting for her on the porch. She climbed onto the small bed and Ben tucked the blankets up around her. He kissed her gently on the cheek, told her he loved her, and turned to leave.

Nina's hand shot out from under the quilt and grabbed his.

"Wait," she said. "Don't go yet. I want to talk to you."

Ben gave her a mischievous grin and sat on the edge of the bed. "Talk, hmmm?" he said, bending forward to kiss her again.

She pushed him back playfully and poked her finger into his chest.

"Yes, *talk.* I want to know what your father was talking about earlier. It sounded like something bad."

Ben sighed and leaned back. His eyes shifted back and forth as he considered his response.

"It's really nothing. Nothing for you to worry about anyway." He leaned forward as if to kiss her again but once more she pushed him away.

"I want to know," she said, obstinate.

"Fine," he said, and sighed again.

"It's just… you have to understand that my parents, and especially my grandparents, they… well, they believe in things that you and I would think are silly, stupid even. It's really just a story."

Nina nodded. She pulled her knees up to her chest, wrapped her arms around them, and told him to go on.

"My family are sheep ranchers. You know this. Well, part of being a rancher is dealing with life and death. Sheep are born, sheep live, sheep die. Sometimes things happen, bad things, which make a lot of them die at once.

"Sometimes it's a drought that means there's not enough food or water. Sometimes it's coyotes that find a weakness in the fence and slaughter a dozen sheep or more in a single night. Sometimes it's a sickness that sweeps through the herd.

"There is one thing which happens which is hard to explain. It must be a disease of some kind, though no one has a name for it or knows why it happens.

"But sometimes the sheep just… well, I can't explain it. Sometimes you go out in the morning and one or two sheep are dead, just lying on the ground. And, well… they're completely drained of blood."

Nina's eyes were wide in the darkness. Ben continued.

"Now, you or I would say this is some disease. This is some sort of… of virus that… I don't know exactly… dehydrates the sheep of their own blood, or something?

"But my parents and grandparents, and many of the old people, they will all say something else. They cannot explain what happens and so they make up monsters to try to make it all make sense."

"Monsters?" Nina asked, shivering despite the warm night.

"What kind of monsters?"

Ben hung his head and laughed.

"Monsters that sneak into the pastures in the dead of night and drain the blood from the sheep."

"Drain their blood? Like vampires?"

Nina knew about vampires; she'd read Dracula when she was in high school.

"Well, yes. Sort of like vampires. But vampires who only like the taste of sheep blood, apparently. Which means that you don't need to worry about it, because last I checked, you are definitely not a sheep."

Nina was quiet for a moment before asking her next question.

"And is this happening now, on your ranch? These sheep that are dying, with all their blood gone?"

Ben nodded his head, an affirmative answer, then placed his hands on Nina's cheeks and looked into her eyes.

"But you do not need to worry about it. It just happens sometimes, for a few weeks or an entire season, and then it stops. We're here for three days, baby, and you've got more important things to focus on than some bloodless sheep.

"Now, no more questions, no more worrying. You need to get some sleep."

He kissed her once, quick but firm, and stood up.

"I'll see you in the morning, baby, and by the end of the day, you'll be Mrs. Nina Lopez."

Nina nodded and stretched out on the bed, doing her best to seem unconcerned. Ben went back into the house.

A single light burned in the hallway beyond, casting an orange rectangle of light onto the smooth floor tiles next to the cot.

Beyond the porch, vast pastureland spread in all directions, and off to the west the mountains rose, vague shadows against a dark sky.

Sounds of nocturnal life thrummed around her: the crickets and the frogs, the occasional distant bleat of a sheep, wind that rustled the tall tufts of grass.

Nina's back ached from two days sitting in the car, and she allowed herself to stretch luxuriously beneath the blankets.

She was fading, halfway between sleep and wakefulness, when she heard a door slam. She raised her head slightly, looking out through the screen.

Around the corner of the house, the back patio was dimly lit by lanterns. Nina lowered her head back to the pillow, held very still, and listened.

There were voices, quiet but distinct: three men. Nina recognized Ben's voice at once, and Leo's slow cadence, and a louder, gruff voice which must be Abuelo.

Ben's voice sounded angry. He was chastising his father for talking about dead sheep in front of Nina.

Leo responded, his words too quiet for Nina to make out.

There was a flurry of conversation, all the men talking at once, their voices rising and falling, the words a knot that Nina could not untangle.

Suddenly Abuelo's gravelly voice rose higher than the others, a command which shut the other two up.

Nina waited.

Abuelo's voice was the only one speaking now. He seemed to be addressing Ben. His words were a mixture of Spanish and English and Nina had to concentrate to make them into coherent sentences.

He berated Ben, complaining about his unbelief.

There was evidence, he said, of the creature. A cave had been found, a cave up in the mountains, where something had been living. It was the creature, he was sure of it, the creature that drains the blood from the sheep.

Something had to be done, they and the other ranchers in the area agreed. They kept an eye on the cave, but the creature had not returned to it. It must have more than one place where it slept.

Already it had taken a dozen of their own sheep. It had to be somewhere still in the area. Something had to be done.

Abuelo finished speaking. Leo's and Ben's voices once again joined in conversation, low murmurings of which Nina could only make out an occasional word.

After a few minutes, a door creaked open, and Regina's voice rang out clear through the night, shooing the men inside, telling them to stop their gossip and get to bed.

Nina lay, alone, in the night.

Overhead the stars moved slowly across the blue-black bowl of the sky. The frog chorus rose and fell and finally faded.

Now and then a stray breeze, warm and gentle, blew across the ranch, reaching into the sleeping porch to lift loose strands of Nina's hair.

Nina slept, exhaustion winning over stress and curiosity, though in her dreams she lay curled up in the midst of a group of sheep which huddled around her, soft and solid, a wall of woolly protection as she watched asteroids streak to earth all around her.

Far off in the darkness, a shrill bleat of alarm lifted into the air and then cut off abruptly.

Nina shifted on the small bed.

Another animal scream sounded, much closer this time, followed by the rumble of a hundred shifting feet seeking escape, and safety.

Nina frowned in her sleep and pulled the blankets up around her chin.

The scuffle of movement, like something which half-walked, half-crawled along the dusty ground just beyond the porch.

Nina's eyes flew open in the darkness.

Only her eyes moved as she looked around, from one corner of the porch to another. She saw nothing. She tried to separate the sounds of her dream from anything she might have heard in the waking world.

A new sound emerged, one which was clearly not a dream: the scratching of nails along wood.

Nina's eyes shot to the door which led from the porch to the world beyond, to the pastures, the mountains, the great wide nothing that surrounded them.

The scratching stopped, as if whatever was making the sound had found what it was searching for. Nina's eyes widened for a fraction of a second as the door began to open, then she squeezed them shut.

Gripping the blankets tight against her cheeks, eyes firmly closed, lips pressed together, Nina's other senses took over and told her all the things she did not wish to know.

The door creaked quietly, slowly open.

The door creaked quietly, slowly closed.

A soft swishing sound as something walked-crawled-dragged itself across the smooth tile of the floor.

The smell that assaulted Nina's nose made her gag, but she willed her body to hold still and the bile to slide back down her throat.

She tilted her head ever-so-slightly so that the quilts pressed against her nostrils, shielding her, at least in part, from the rank odor. It smelled of mud and rotting vegetation, unwashed bodies and wet dog, and above all these came the sharp and unmistakable metallic tang of blood.

Nina wanted to move. She wanted to leap from her bed and burst through the door into the house.

She wanted to scream, to call for help, to yell Ben's name and to shriek wordlessly at the top of her lungs.

There was a terrifying creak and a shifting of the wood at the end of her small camp bed.

She felt the thin mattress depress somewhere below her feet, the familiar sensation of someone sitting at the end of the bed.

For a briefly ecstatic moment, Nina considered the idea that it might be Ben, come to surprise her, or even to scare her with a little joke. But no. Ben would never smell like that.

The blankets shifted, pulled taut against the place where she gripped them in claw-like hands. Cool air drifted in around her feet as the quilts were lifted and it - the thing - whatever it was - crawled beneath them.

Nina could feel the shifting of the thing's body as it curled up just inches from her bare feet.

Hot, moist breath filled the space at the bottom of the bed.

And then a snuffling sound. The thing was smelling her.

Nina's heart pounded erratically as the creature's long, dry, leathery fingers touched her feet, her ankles, the long hard bones of her shins.

Please no, please no, no more, she begged, silent words which repeated in an endless loop inside her head.

The snuffling sound grew louder as the thing pressed its nose-muzzle-snout against the sensitive skin on the soles of her feet.

A heavy, dizzying blackness, darker than the backs of her eyelids, overwhelmed her. The blood rushed in her ears and she bit down hard on her lip to keep from moaning.

The snuffling stopped. The creature's hands slipped slowly, gently, away from her legs. It shifted once more, like a dog turning in circles before lying down to sleep, and then seemed to settle.

Time slowed to a crawl.

Nina's muscles ached, spasmed, and went numb. Blood welled along her bottom lip where her teeth sank into it again and again, keeping back the noises which would wake the thing which slept at the foot of her bed.

Hours passed, hours which could have been minutes or years. Nina's heart rate slowed; from a pounding frenzy it dropped into its regular rhythm, then reduced even further as if Nina were trying to stop the blood from flowing within her body altogether.

As time passed, her eyes drifted slowly open, staring directly ahead of her at the rectangles of night framed by the porch windows.

Slowly, the black sky took on an indigo hue, which lightened to navy blue.

Nina's pupils contracted as the first rays of the sun broke across the land.

Nina sucked in a small gasp of air through her nose as she heard the first sounds of life within the house.

The thing at the foot of her bed shifted slightly, and made a sound which was part whimper, part growl, then settled back into a softly-snoring slumber.

Nina did not move. She did not scream. She was utterly frozen, paralyzed by fear.

The calm, quiet terror of the night seemed suddenly favorable to the surreal feeling of the morning, where the dawn light trickled over the land and the normal sounds of people waking within the house made the reality of her situation that much more unnerving.

Footsteps approached through the house, coming closer and closer to the porch. Nina took small, quick breaths. The door just beside her head thumped against the wall as Regina stepped out.

"Still in bed –" Regina's voice trailed off, a look of confusion and concern on her face as she looked into Nina's terrified eyes.

Then Regina's sight was drawn to the strange shifting shape at the end of the bed, her mouth opening in horror as Nina felt the blankets fall flat against her legs once more.

Regina let out a raw, throaty scream as the pale creature slid from beneath the blankets and rushed toward the door, running on all fours like a dog though it was shaped more like a man.

The sound of her future mother-in-law's cry released the shriek that had been hiding in Nina's chest all night long, and her own high, hysterical wail joined Regina's deeper shout.

Nina shot up in bed, kicking the soiled blankets away from her, drawing her knees up to her chest and pressing her back against the wall.

Through the screened windows the women watched as the creature scurried-ran-crawled across the ground, making its way toward the mountains in the distance.

Men's shouts rose to their right as Ben, Leo, and Abuelo rushed after it in pursuit.

The creature was incredibly fast, there was no way the men could catch it, but as Regina pulled Nina into her arms and their screams died to whimpers, something flew through the air.

It flashed in the glare of the morning sun as it spun over and over itself, arcing toward the creature.

They heard the thud as the weapon found its mark.

The creature let out a howl and fell; it seemed to convulse there on the ground, noises beyond description rising from its mouth.

For a moment, all was still.

The men stopped in their tracks. Regina held Nina's face against her bosom, shielding her from the horror. Then a cry went up from the men, a cry of triumph, and they raced toward the creature which lay now, completely still, a pale shape against the dirt.

Nina and Regina watched, speechless, as the men crowded around the thing on the ground. They gesticulated wildly, mouths moving quickly though their words were caught and flung away on the wind.

Ben was sent to fetch a wheelbarrow from the barn; Abuelo returned to the house and was immediately on the phone, calling every other rancher in the area.

Leo stood watch over the creature alone, and after staring at it for a moment, he knelt down and pulled his machete from the back of the thing's skull.

He looked at the blood that lined the blade, a pale red that dripped thinly from the tip. He made a small grunt of disgust in his throat and wiped the weapon back and forth across a nearby tuft of drying grass before sliding it back into the leather holster that hung from his belt.

Ben returned with the wheelbarrow and an old moth-eaten blanket. Together the two men lifted the body into the barrow and covered it, then wheeled it slowly and carefully back behind the house.

Nina was still sitting on the bed, backed against the wall, Regina's hands fluttering nervously over her in a helpless maternal way, when Ben finally stepped out onto the porch.

His eyes flitted back and forth from his fiancé to his mother, brows furrowed. His mother nodded encouragingly at him and left back the way she had come, back into the house.

Ben knelt before Nina on the floor and took her hands. They were cold despite the quickly warming temperature of the day. He rubbed them gently for a moment, then used his hands to turn her face toward him.

Nina looked at him blankly for a moment. A harsh shudder traveled through her entire body and she gasped as if just waking from a nightmare.

Her eyes focused on Ben's face, and her own face crumpled. She fell against him, an awkward angle that pained her cramped muscles, but she didn't care.

Tears streamed down her face and soaked his shirt as he wrapped his arms around her shoulders and made quiet shushing noises.

A soft knock on the door made them both look up. Regina stood there with an older man behind her.

"Ah," Ben said, and he gently lifted Nina away from him. "The doctor is here, Nina. Let him look at you."

Nina consented to a quick examination, after which the doctor proclaimed her perfectly healthy and physically unharmed, though obviously in shock.

"But what about—" Ben began, and his mother gave him a sharp look.

"What about what?" the doctor asked.

"Well," Ben said, glancing nervously toward Nina in a curious way, "what about her hair?"

"My hair?" Nina asked, confused, and she reached up carefully to make sure her long locks were still there.

"Her hair?" asked the doctor, also confused.

"What about it?"

Regina sighed and pulled from the voluminous pocket of her apron a small mirror. She handed it to Nina, letting her hand rest reassuringly on Nina's shoulder for a moment before stepping back.

Nina looked from Ben to his mother to the doctor and back again.

"What about my hair?" she asked again, her hands shaking as they held the mirror.

"Just look, *mija*," Regina said quietly, with a sad smile.

Nina lifted the mirror up in front of her face. She let her eyes slide sideways until she looked at her own reflection.

She gasped, one hand over her mouth as the other swung the mirror from side to side to take it all in.

Her long black hair had turned stark white.

Back in the classroom

The students sat, open-mouthed and speechless. Finally, Brian Graff found his voice: "So… like, fear…"

Mrs. Lopez nodded. "Yes, Brian. Fear. Fear had turned my hair white, and it's never gone back."

"But what *was* the thing that… well, what was the thing? What did they do with it? Did you still get married that day? Were there more of whatever that was?"

The teacher smiled, crossed her arms across her chest, and leaned back.

"The thing – the creature that drained the blood from the sheep – well, I don't know exactly what to call it. Before mid-morning every rancher in the area had arrived at the Lopez ranch to see it. They kept it in one of the many outbuildings behind the house. After a while I even went out to look at it, though my heart pounded the entire time.

"It was partly a man, and partly an animal. It was short – maybe five feet tall, but with long gangly arms and legs that let it run like a dog. Its face was barely human, but human just the same.

"It was completely white, pale like the slugs that live beneath rotted wood. Even its lips were pale, and its eyes were pink. It had only a few teeth, yellow and rotted, but its canines were especially long and sharp. All over its body it had cuts and bruises, and a rash of crusty sores that must have caused it constant pain.

"Later that day, after everyone had come to see the creature and then returned to their own homes, Leo and Abuelo took the body up into the mountains and burned it. I don't know if there were any more. I don't know if it was human, animal, hybrid, or some strange new creature never before discovered.

"We were not married that day. In the chaos and confusion, I knew only one thing for certain: that I wanted to go home.

"Ben obliged, packing all our things back into the car, and we drove away while a disappointed but understanding Regina waved from the door. We were married here in town, by the Justice of the Peace. And then, life went on, perfectly normal, just as it had always done."

The bell rang, signaling the start of summer, but Mrs. Lopez's class moved sluggishly, gathering their bags and whispering to one another as they passed slowly out of the classroom.

Brian Graff was the last one out, and he stopped to speak once more.

"That was some story, Mrs. Lopez. I – I hope you have a nice summer. Got any exciting plans?"

Nina Lopez smiled and shook her head.

"My husband, Ben, goes back for a few weeks every summer to visit his parents on their ranch. But I'll be at home. I don't go back there. I won't ever go back there."

Brian nodded once, unsure of what to say, and walked away.

Nina took in a deep breath, held it for a moment, and blew it back out. Then she turned, brushed her long white hair away from her face, and began gathering up her things.

Two Heads are Better than One

Jonas stared down at his hands, covered in blood.

He stared at the crimson pool which stopped just short of his shiny black shoes.

He ran a hand through his hair, more orange than red, so that it stood up on his head like a hundred tiny flames.

He kept his eyes on the body in front of him, but he could feel the other one there, right next to him, just beyond the edge of his sight.

Jonas sniffled and wiped a hand across his mouth, leaving bloody fingerprints on his cheeks.

"This is your fault," he said, "It's all your fault."

The other one simply laughed.

Jonas let his eyes wander around the shadowy mill until they settled on the band saw in the far corner. He set his jaw, squared his shoulders, and started toward it.

One week earlier

Jonas was weeping.

He knew it wasn't manly to cry. He cursed himself even as the tears fell. He paced back and forth through his small apartment, and he pounded his fists against the walls until the neighbors pounded back and yelled for him to knock it off already.

His heart was broken and his dreams were crushed and there was just so much pain inside him that he could not contain it and it came out in tears and groans and great shuddering sobs.

He had seen them together, Emily and Jim Pennington, seen them arm in arm as they walked through town, seen the way she smiled up at him and laughed and the way Jim's arm crept slowly around her perfect tiny waist and the way his fingers brushed back a stray hair from her face.

Emily. *His* Emily.

Jonas threw himself across his bed and beat the mattress with his hands. He muffled his shouts in his pillow until he ran out of energy to shout with.

He lay on the bed, staring wordlessly up at the ceiling as the daylight beyond the windows fell away and darkness rose to take its place. He thought about Emily, and he thought about Jim, and the more he thought, the more angry he felt. His anger, however, was weak, impotent. A hundred visions of violence flashed through his mind, but he knew he could never follow through on them.

All his life he'd been the weak one, the quiet one, the frail one, the boy who loved books more than athletics, science more than socializing.

Emily had been the first to really see him, to look beyond his scrawny arms and pale skin and see the intellect within. He had seized upon this unexpected attention and given his own affection back in unreserved amounts.

He had loved Emily O'Hanlon from that very first day, loved her truly, unconditionally, uncontrollably.

And now she was stepping out with Jim Pennington.

Jonas rolled back and forth in his sweat-soaked sheets as if in a fever, half-asleep, half-delirious, cursing Jim Pennington in low mumblings and wishing every harm he could imagine upon him, until finally exhaustion took him and he slept.

The sun shone brightly through the window when he cracked his eyes open the next morning. It wasn't the sun that had awoken him, but a persistent itch upon his right shoulder.

He scratched and scratched at it, undoing the top buttons of his shirt so he could slide his hand inside and scratch some more, until his fingers came away red with blood.

Jonas sat up, staring at the bloodstain. He stood and made his way across the bedroom to the tiny closet that served as a bathroom.

Over the sink hung an old mirror, black around the edges and missing a sliver of glass in one corner. Jonas stripped off his shirt and looked at his reflection, twisting his arm this way and that as he looked for the cause of the incessant itching.

All the mirror showed were the bloody score-marks where his own fingernails had dug into his skin.

It was probably nothing, he decided. Perhaps a mosquito had managed to get inside his collar and bite him repeatedly. At worst it might be a spider bite, but even that didn't worry him too much.

The truth was, he was too tired and too despondent to spare much care for this mysterious itch.

The small clock on his bureau read ten minutes to eight, so Jonas quickly bandaged up his shoulder, pulled on a clean shirt, ran a damp comb through his hair, and hurried out of his apartment.

He rushed down the steep side stairs and up the dusty street to the enormous building which sat at the far end of town: O'Hanlon's Lumber Mill.

The idea that he might not show up to work on this particular day, the day after his boss's daughter had broken his heart without even knowing it, had never occurred to Jonas.

Routine and structure were the glue which held his life together, and that he might simply quit his job and get as far away as possible from Emily O'Hanlon and the pain she'd caused him was a concept which his brain could not begin to comprehend.

Jonas entered through the wide front doors of the mill and turned immediately to the left.

Off to the right was the enormous room where the logs were cut, trimmed, or pulped, a room full of dangerous machines and dangerous men. Jonas himself worked within the administrative wing of the building, in a tiny office with only one small circular window located high up on the wall, a window which let in sunlight but afforded Jonas no view of the outside world; here he kept the books and made sure that every penny that came in or out of the mill was accounted for.

He closed the door behind him, dampening the sounds of the saws and the raucous laughter and dirty jokes of the men on the other side of the mill.

Most of the men would be loading up in the company's three huge trucks for the trek to the other side of nearby Blackjack Mountain, where they would spend the day felling trees to feed the mill.

The morning passed slowly. At one point, Jonas thought he could make out the sound of Emily's laughter somewhere in the building. She sometimes came to visit her father as Frank O'Hanlon sat giving orders in his own office – much larger and more richly appointed than Jonas's, and with windows on three walls.

Normally Jonas would find some reason to talk to Mr. O'Hanlon when he heard that sound, on the off chance that he might cross paths with Emily and feel the radiant warmth of her smile.

Not today.

Jonas did not budge from his chair for the rest of the day, not even when the noon whistle blew. He worked through the hours, trying his best to keep his mind focused on the ledgers in front of him and off the thought of Jim Pennington's hands on Emily's waist.

Jonas's right hand scribbled column after column of numbers as his left hand, almost without conscious thought, rubbed and scratched at the insufferable itch on his shoulder.

As the clock ticked over to five o'clock, Jonas leaned back in his chair, stretched his cramped muscles, and winced at a sharp pain in that same shoulder, like someone had just opened a gash in his skin.

He patted at his shirt with one hand, but no blood came away on his fingers, so he shrugged, stood, gathered his things, and left the building.

After a dinner of slightly stale bread and some cheese just on the cusp of going moldy, washed down with tepid water from the bathroom sink, Jonas slid his arms out of his shirt, intending to slip into his pajamas and try to distract himself with a book until he was tired enough to sleep.

He gasped as the shirt slid to the floor.

His shoulder was an angry red, and he twisted so that the top of the shoulder cap faced the mirror.

With one finger he touched the perfect oval of inflamed skin, and nearly passed out when the skin split widthwise down the center of the oval.

There was no blood, and only a little pain; the thing which made Jonas sway where he stood was the way the wound looked at him, for as the skin peeled apart, he could swear that something peered out from the tissue within, something that looked alarmingly like a very small eye.

Jonas looked away, stared at the floor for several long moments, forcing himself to breathe slowly and deeply before daring to look once more toward his own shoulder.

He jumped back at what he saw. Sure enough, the skin seemed to open and close like an eyelid, and from within something reflected the overhead light.

He tilted his shoulder toward the mirror again, and it was undeniable: an eye, half the size of his own but the exact same pale shade of blue, looked up at him from within its fleshy lids.

Jonas gripped the sides of the sink to keep from passing out. His brain could not process this. It could not be real. A thought passed through his mind and he latched onto it like a drowning man to a life preserver: it wasn't real.

He was hallucinating. He had been under too much stress in the last two days, hadn't slept well, had barely eaten. His mind was just overworked.

It wasn't real.

Jonas helped himself to a large quantity of whiskey before resolutely buttoning up his pajama shirt, refusing to let himself even glance toward his shoulder.

He slept surprisingly well, all things considered.

So well that when he first woke up, his head still slightly fuzzy from the whiskey, his mind was blessedly free of the memory of both Emily's betrayal and the strange discovery of the night before.

It was quite a shock to him, then, when he went to dress for work and discovered there were now *two* pale blue eyes staring up at the ceiling from his shoulder.

Jonas threw back another tumblerful of whiskey, wrapped a generous amount of gauze over his shoulder, covering the eyes, and dressed for work.

As he walked down the street to the mill, he repeated this mantra in his head: it's not real, it's not real, it's not real.

All day long as he worked he had the strangest sensation in his right shoulder, a slight fluttering, and his heart pained him as he realized the feeling was most closely akin to the sensation he felt against his neck when Emily laid her head against him and her eyelashes fluttered daintily against his skin.

As he walked home at the end of the day, he repeated again: it's not real, it's not real, it's not real.

Jonas threw back two glasses of whiskey before he worked up the courage to take off his shirt and unwrap the sweaty bandages.

He let out a strangled scream. Two blue eyes. The tip of a nose. Two lips, sealed shut.

Jonas passed out on the bathroom floor.

When he woke, all was quiet and dark. He refused to turn up the gas lamps, refused to look in the mirror.

All he would allow himself to do was crawl to his bed and sink once more into the oblivion of sleep.

Jonas had some thinking to do, when he went to get dressed the next morning.

Two eyes, a nose, a mouth, slightly open, something darting around inside, disturbingly like a tongue. And the whole thing was raised up off his shoulder in a mound roughly three inches tall.

He could not hide that under bandages and a shirt.

Jonas went to work that day with an enormous scarf wrapped around his neck and shoulders. He told anyone who asked that he was feeling under the weather, coming down with a bad cold.

A persistent ache in his shoulder throughout the day made him scared to remove the scarf, even when he had returned home and locked himself away in the privacy of his own rooms that evening.

The bulge had grown, had separated itself from his shoulder so that it sat atop it now like a fleshy boulder, connected by a thinner piece of muscle that resembled nothing so much as a neck.

A fuzz of wild red-orange hair spread across the top of the growth. The eyes blinked at Jonas in the mirror. The mouth opened and closed like a fish gasping for air.

Jonas drank the rest of the bottle of whiskey and laid down on his bed.

He woke in the darkness to the sound of whispering. He stiffened where he lay, trying to discern where the voice came from. It sounded like it was in the room with him.

It sounded as if it were in the bed, right next to him. With a sense of foreboding dread, Jonas turned his head slowly to the right. His nose bumped into the nose of the thing which had grown upon his shoulder, and as the whispers continued, he felt the breath of the thing's mouth as it spoke.

"It's not real, it's not real, it's not real," Jonas repeated to himself.

"Oh, it's real, buddy."

The voice was not a whisper anymore. It sounded almost identical to his own voice, only rougher somehow, the speech less refined.

Jonas looked with horror into the eyes of the thing that lay next to him on the pillow.

The head laughed.

"Come on, buddy. How can you think I'm not real? You're looking right at me, ain't you?"

Jonas stared.

"You think I'm… what? A hallucination? Oh, yeah, cause you've lost your damn mind over that girl, am I right?

"Well, guess what, buddy? I'm real as they come, and I'm gonna help you get your girl back."

Despite the utter insanity of what was happening, a thrill raced through Jonas's heart at the idea of Emily back in his arms, far away from that blundering fool Jim Pennington.

"H-How?" Jonas asked, afraid of the answer even as he said the word.

"Never you mind, buddy. You just go to sleep and leave it to me. That's it, now, back to sleep. Rock-a-bye-baby and all that."

Jonas knitted his eyebrows in confusion for a moment before a peaceful sleepiness descended over him. His eyes closed. The other eyes remained wide open.

The other mouth laughed aloud in the darkness.

The next morning Jonas awoke to a commotion in the street below his window. He pulled back the curtains and looked out, careful to stay hidden from view.

A small crowd gathered in the middle of the road. From down the street the sheriff came running, still buckling his gun belt around his considerable waist.

"Stand back, stand back!" the sheriff yelled, and the crowd scattered and revealed the thing that had attracted so much attention.

Jonas gasped in shock. A body lay in the street, covered in blood. The face was turned away from him, but Jonas recognized the profile.

"Jim Pennington," he whispered, then turned with wide eyes to the thing upon his shoulder.

"What did you do?" he said, his voice barely audible.

The thing winked one eye and said, "Helped you out, buddy boy. Got rid of the competition, as it were. You can thank me later. Right now, I need a little shut-eye."

It closed its eyes and leaned its head against Jonas's neck, and a shudder of revulsion crawled down Jonas's spine at the contact.

He didn't know what else to do, so he dressed, pointedly ignoring the small amounts of blood that still stained his sink and crusted beneath his fingernails.

He scrubbed his hands hard and wrapped the scarf around himself once more and headed down the street to work.

Within the mill conversation was subdued. The machines were still and silent. Jonas kept his head down as he headed to his own office and closed the door with a sigh of relief.

He had worked for less than an hour when a sharp knock on the door was followed immediately by Nancy Fulton, Mr. O'Hanlon's secretary, opening it and sticking her head in through the gap.

"Go on home, Jonas," she said. "Mill's closed for the day on account of what happened."

"Oh," Jonas said, and then again, "Oh."

Nancy looked him over curiously. "You doing Okay, Jonas? You don't look so good. Maybe that cold of yours is a bit more serious than you think."

Jonas sat up straighter in his chair and did his best to smile. "Oh, no, Nancy, I'm fine. Just a little sick and um… maybe a little shocked by… by the day's events."

Nancy gave Jonas a sad smile and nodded her head.

"A terrible thing, it is, and Mr. O'Hanlon has his hands full for sure, what with one of his best workers gone and poor Emily in quite a state. Mr. O'Hanlon had just given his approval to young Jim yesterday, you know."

Jonas looked up at her with incomprehension. "His approval? For what?"

Nancy laughed, then caught herself and arranged her face into one more appropriate for the day.

"Why, for Jim to marry Miss Emily, of course!"

Jonas's own face must have shown something of his true feelings in that moment, for a sudden comprehension dawned on Nancy's own features as she looked at him.

"Oh, Jonas. Oh, sweetie."

She laid a hand gently on his left shoulder and he jerked away from her.

"Oh, I never knew you had it so bad. It would never have worked, though, darlin'. Mr. O'Hanlon would never approve. He needs a son-in-law strong enough to carry on the family business, you know.

"And you… you've got a good head for numbers and all, Jonas, but he'd never have let you marry his daughter."

She gave him one last sympathetic look as she left.

Jonas sat quietly at his desk for a few minutes before standing to leave. A muffled sound came from inside the scarf, but he ignored it.

He walked down the street as if in a trance, back to his rooms, his small haven of safety.

He went to the bathroom, stood in front of the mirror, and unwound the scarf. The top three buttons of his shirt were already undone to allow room for the head. It stared at him in the mirror.

"Aw, don't look so glum, buddy. If Daddy dearest is all that stands in the way, just leave it to me."

Jonas said nothing. He went back to the bedroom and pulled a brand-new bottle of whiskey from the shelf.

He drank the whole thing and let the blackness of oblivion descend.

A scream rent the night.

Jonas sat up in bed, arms and legs twitching. Outside, the pale light of the moon lit the town. No one moved, not a single person was in sight as he looked out the window.

Jonas looked frantically up and down the street.

The lights were on in the mill. Jonas grappled with his own pants until he extricated his pocket watch. Three in the morning.

A horrible feeling rippled through his gut.

He stood and stumbled drunkenly out the door, down the stairs – nearly falling and breaking his own neck twice – and ran down the street toward the mill.

The door was unlocked, the light from within spilling out through the high windows onto the ground outside. Jonas entered silently. To his left, the sound of a woman sobbing made his stomach clench.

It was Emily, he was sure of it.

He followed the sound to the big office in the back. Mr. O'Hanlon's office. He pushed the door open gently.

There, on the floor, Emily had thrown herself over her father's body. Mr. O'Hanlon's neck was ringed with purple bruises in the shape of fingers, and Jonas felt his own hands twitch at the sight. Emily's entire body shook with her sobs.

"Emily?" Jonas said, and she turned suddenly with a gasp of fright.

"Oh, Jonas!" she said, wiping tears from her face. "Oh, Jonas, help! Oh…"

Her eyes drifted from Jonas's face to the thing upon his shoulder. Horror crept across her features. Emily scrambled to her feet and backed away to the wall furthest from him. Her arm raised shakily, one finger pointing.

"Jonas," she said, and her voice trembled, "what is that?"

Jonas, in his rush, had all but forgotten it… him — the other.

He put his hands out as if to assure Emily that he meant her no harm.

"Let me explain," he said, but Emily was already skirting around him, her back pressed against the walls as she made her way to the door.

"Emily!" Jonas called as she darted through the open doorway mere feet away from him.

He followed her, the sound of her footsteps echoing loudly as she ran into the cavernous mill.

The great hulking machines made the room a maze through which he ran, Emily's skirts always swishing around a corner just a little ahead of him.

Finally, he found her crouching in a corner, her hands over her face, her entire body shaking. Jonas knelt in front of her, grasped her arms, pulled her up.

She resisted, refusing to look at him. A scream rose in her throat and Jonas clamped one hand over her mouth before it could escape.

"Emily," he panted, spinning her around so that her back was to his chest and his arms wrapped tightly around her.

"Emily, I'm so sorry, but don't you see? Now we can be together! Now no one can stop us! That idiot Jim is out of the way, and your father can't protest the marriage, so we can… we can be together.

"Doesn't that make you happy?"

Emily bit the inside of the hand he held over her mouth and he jerked it away, cursing.

She spun out of his grasp and stood facing him, disgust and hatred changing her beautiful face into something ugly and monstrous.

"Marry you?" She laughed, wild and loud.

"Why would I ever want to do that? It's Jim Pennington I loved, you imbecile! I would never have married you!"

She glared at him, her eyes darting back and forth between Jonas and the *other*, which kept its mouth closed but shifted slightly back and forth on Jonas's shoulder.

Tears streamed down Jonas's face and a blush of shame rose to his cheeks.

"You would… but I thought…"

Emily laughed again. "You thought what? That I loved you? Oh, you silly little boy! Why would I want you when I could have a real man like Jim?"

Jonas saw red, a bloody haze that descended over his vision like fog.

He felt his arms stretch out toward Emily, heard her laughter cut short, felt the tender flesh of her throat beneath his fingers, heard the gasping of her breath and felt the beating of her fists against his chest, felt the blows weaken.

He felt himself turning her body in his arms, felt his hand slip into his pocket, saw the glint of the light on his pocketknife as he opened it.

Felt the hot spurt of her blood as it cascaded from her newly-opened throat.

He stepped back. Emily's body fell to the floor, a dull thud that echoed through the mill.

Jonas stared down at his hands, covered in blood.

He stared at the crimson pool which stopped just short of his shiny black shoes.

He ran a hand through his hair, more orange than red, so that it stood up on his head like a hundred tiny flames.

He kept his eyes on the body in front of him, but he could feel the other one there, right next to him, just beyond the edge of his sight.

Jonas sniffled and wiped a hand across his mouth, leaving bloody fingerprints on his cheeks.

"This is your fault," he said. "It's all your fault."

The other one simply laughed.

Jonas let his eyes wander around the shadowy mill until they settled on the band saw in the far corner.

He set his jaw, squared his shoulders and started toward it. He flipped the switch on the side and the saw roared to noisy life.

Jonas gripped the sides of the machine, leaning forward, closer to the saw, closer and closer. The thing on his shoulder rocked back and forth frantically, making sounds that were more animal than human.

Jonas took a deep breath. He could feel the heat of the saw; its movement was a thunderous vibration in his ears. He lined things up as best he could, closed his eyes, and forced his body forward.

The pain as the saw cut through the muscles attaching the thing to his shoulder was unfathomable.

The thing screamed. Jonas screamed.

The second head fell to the ground, spurting blood into the sawdust.

Jonas tried to stand, stumbled, slid sideways. The saw band chewed through skin, muscle, tendon bone.

When the men came into work the next day, the band saw still buzzed quietly in its corner and the air reeked with the coppery scent of blood.

It didn't take long to discover why. Someone went running for the sheriff.

By the day's end, three bodies and one curiously shaped chunk of wood – one which reminded the men eerily of a miniature head and which was covered with Jonas Holt's blood – had been removed from the mill.

The sheriff was so disturbed by the hunk of wood after a few days of staring at it that he refused to keep it in his office any longer, instead slipping back into the mill under cover of darkness to deposit the accursed object on a desk in the small, unused office that had once belonged to Jonas Holt.

Leaderless, the men who had worked for O'Hanlon slowly disappeared from town. The mill was shut down, its doors locked, its machines silenced.

Though there are some, even today, that say that if you venture close to the mill at night and press your ear to the wall just below a high circular window, you can hear a low, chuckling laugh echoing within.

SAFE HOUSE

I hadn't been back to my grandfather's place in thirty years. I spent a good deal of time there as a child, visiting on most holidays and spending weeks at a time during the summers.

My grandpa owned several acres of land which surrounded a house he'd designed himself. Mostly it was farmland and open prairieland, knee-high grasses undulating like ocean waves as far as the eye could see.

My grandfather died when I was ten years old. Since my mother was not particularly fond of Granny, who was Grandpa's second wife, we never returned to his place after the funeral.

I was too young to understand the complexities in my mom's relationship with her stepmother; I only knew that we couldn't go back to the house that held so many wonderful memories. So, in my child's mind, I made Granny the villain. She got Grandpa's house and we didn't.

Something of my mother's dislike for her took root inside my own heart.

Thirty years passed. Granny lived to the ripe old age of ninety-three before passing away in her sleep. Her home health nurse found her in bed, looking peaceful but decidedly dead, when she came for one of her twice-weekly visits.

I couldn't really find it in my heart to work up any grief over her passing. I hadn't spared her much thought for three decades.

I didn't attend the funeral. But I did attend the reading of the will.

Imagine my surprise upon finding that per my grandfather's will, when Granny died, the entire property passed to my mother. Well, my mother passed away four years ago, so according to some legal jargon the lawyer attempted rather unsuccessfully to explain, the property then passed to my brother and me.

That is how I found myself driving along a lonely country road on a late November afternoon, storm clouds gathering on the western horizon.

I had never driven this way myself. I had, of course, been a child in the backseat of my parents' car every time I had come before. I had a memory of long straight stretches of roads that were barely more than dirt paths between farmers' fields.

My memory wasn't far from the truth.

By the miracle that is GPS, I navigated along back roads with names like 'County Road 10490' and 'Bob's Road' until the familiar wooden fencing came into view.

I had not been to this house in thirty years, not in real life, but I had visited many times in my dreams. I have always been a vivid dreamer, and in childhood and adolescence, almost every single nightmare I had ended with me running to this house to find safety.

My subconscious mind had turned it into a literal safe place. Memory upon happy golden memory of my time at that house, that property, had piled up in my brain.

Lazy summer days reading Laura Ingalls Wilder. Picking berries, entirely inedible but fun to hunt just the same, a small basket slung over my arm and the sun warm on my shoulders.

Searching out bird nests in the trees that surrounded the property. Skipping out to my grandfather's shop where he whittled away at bits of wood and made furniture for my dollhouse.

Christmases in the huge living room, a tree decorated entirely in red ornaments. Memories to banish the creatures and fears that filled a young girl's dreams.

Perhaps because I had held the house so dearly in my dreams, my memory of it fit surprisingly well with the reality of the place my car now sat idling in front of.

A long drive lined on both sides by tall, thin poplars led to a low house painted in cream and brown so that it blended in with the autumn landscape.

I pulled into the circle drive and shut the car off.

It took me a few moments to work up the nerve to step out of the car. The house looked shabbier up close, with peeling paint and loose window screens. Well, Granny had been ninety-three. She probably hadn't been out painting the house the week she died.

I grabbed my overnight bag from the backseat and approached the front door. Set back in a narrow recess, I stood in shadows as I stabbed the key around the lock until it finally slid home.

The door, a giant, heavy, multi-paneled monstrosity of yellow 1970s wood, swung inward silently.

A memory jolted through me then, of the screen door that used to be there. Once when I was five years old, I'd gotten excited upon seeing a turtle out on the sidewalk, and in my hurry to run in and tell everyone else, had managed to slam my thumb in that screen door.

A trip to the emergency room had followed, and though my thumb wasn't broken, the thumbnail had fallen off, the skin beneath wrinkled and bruised.

I shuddered at the unpleasant memory.

Inside, I fumbled for a light switch. Funny that I had spent so much time here as a child and yet had no idea where the switch was.

When I finally located it, a dim yellow light flickered on overhead, illuminating a short but narrow hallway. I felt like I could probably navigate this house with my eyes closed, relying entirely on memory, but I flipped lights on as I went just the same.

The entry hall opened on the left into the huge living room, with tall windows facing the front yard. Behind the living room, facing the back yard, was an enormous country kitchen with white cabinets and a wide bar that my brother and I had sat at to eat more times than I could count.

Beyond the kitchen, another short hallway, and then the master suite. As a child I'd thought this room worthy of royalty. It was easily the largest bedroom I've ever been in, with an en-suite bathroom complete with hot tub and – of all things – swinging saloon doors.

I stepped into the bedroom, flipped the light switch and – nothing. The bulb must have burnt out.

The light of the setting sun filtered in around the edges of the heavy drapes which covered an entire wall of windows. I pulled one panel back, ran my fingers along the fabric, thick pea-green stuff, probably the same drapes which had hung here when I was a child.

The massive king-sized bed was certainly the same, with intricately carved woodwork on the headboard, and behind it a wallpaper I would never forget.

Stretching along that entire wall, the wallpaper formed a scene of faded green-gray tree trunks, like you could walk straight from the bedroom into a somewhat sickly forest. I ran my fingers along the wall, tracing the skeletal trunk of a tree. I always had thought that wallpaper a strange choice, even as a little girl.

I sat on the edge of the bed. Someone had stripped the bedclothes off, leaving only a stained beige mattress.

My stomach clenched around the memory of my grandfather lying in this bed, his body wasted away to nothingness by the cancer that ate at his insides, spreading from one vital organ to another.

I remembered how tightly he'd gripped my hand, how the baseball cap he'd worn had fitted too loosely and had shifted back and forth as he'd swiveled his head against the pillows.

I was holding the edge of the mattress as though it was his hand, although this time it was my own grip that was tight. I felt a sudden urge to get out of the room, a thousand pinprick goosebumps starting at my shoulders and rushing down to my feet.

I shivered, just noticing the chill which must have been in the air the whole time. It was November, after all, and the heating in the empty house had probably been turned off.

I closed the door to the master bedroom firmly behind me when I left. I passed back through the living room and the entry hall.

Down a long, lightless hallway to the right of the entry were two doors. The one on the right led to my uncle's old bedroom, where my brother had always stayed, the one on the left to my aunt's old room, which had been my home away from home when we visited.

I opened the door to this room and was assaulted with the musty odor of a space long neglected. I guess old Granny didn't have much use for this end of the house. There was no telling when someone had last aired out these rooms.

When I turned the light on, I was overcome with a feeling of such overwhelming familiarity that it took my breath away.

Tears sprung to my eyes as I looked around at a room utterly unchanged since the last time I saw it. The white four-poster bed with posts that reached almost to the ceiling still sat in one corner, the green and white flowered bedspread tucked neatly around it.

The white chair with the wickerwork back where I'd stacked my clothes. The bathroom beyond, and the walk-in closet that had held such wondrous treasures.

The room had only one window, and I pulled back the yellowed drapes which covered it. An overgrown bush obscured the bottom half of the window, but out the top half I could see my car just off to the right.

The storm clouds which had been miles away when I'd arrived were now much closer, the sun a barely visible orange glow near the horizon, minutes away from disappearing. A great fork of lightning lit the sky, blue-white against the darkening clouds.

A loud humming made me step back from the window, then a loud click and a blinding light shined directly in my face. I had forgotten the outdoor lights, which sat outside each window and lit the house up at night, making it a forlorn and lonely structure glowing on the endless flat expanse of dark farmland that surrounded it.

I don't know how I could have forgotten the lights. They had been a source of comfort to me as a little girl, curled up alone in that big four poster bed, with all the adults in the house sleeping in rooms at each far end, seemingly miles worth of distance to a child at night. There had been one time, though …

I was eight years old, woken from a sound sleep by a sudden noise, a thump outside the window. In my half-asleep state, it had taken me a moment to realize that the room was far darker than it should have been.

The light beyond the window was out, the room so dark I could barely see my hand in front of my face. Every noise seemed magnified, the wind in the grasses beyond the window, the scritch-scratch of the bush against the windowpane, my own breathing, and my heartbeat thudding in my ears.

I had screamed, or cried out, or made some sort of noise, because within moments my mother was there, my grandfather close on her heels.

Grandpa had assured me that the bulb had just gone out in that particular light, that they would replace it the next day.

He'd moved to pull the curtains back to show me that all the other lights were still on, but I'd cried out for him not to. I knew, somewhere deep in my gut, with the certainty borne of childhood faith, that to open the curtains would be to invite the darkness and whatever dwelt within it into my room.

In my mind's eye I pictured a huge wolf, with fur the color of a bruise and beady red eyes that glowed in the darkness.

In the present, as I sat, an adult alone in the house with a storm moving in, the memory made an icy current of fear wash over me.

Strange that I had forgotten that night. Remembering it now, it had a surreal dream-like quality to it. Perhaps I had actually dreamed the whole thing.

Certainly, I had slept in that room many times after that night without fear. Hadn't I?

I had not slept there that particular night that; I know. My mother, sensing my dread, had allowed me to sleep with her in the room at the far end of the hall, the room which wasn't actually just a room but rather an entire separate living space tacked on to the main house.

When my grandfather bought this property and began living on it, he had first built a simple home, a large rectangular structure made of prefabricated pieces.

Within that rectangle was a large living room, larger even than the one in the main house, with the back third of the structure containing, all in a row, a bedroom, a bathroom, another bedroom, and then a small kitchen which was open to the living room.

When his business had become successful and money wasn't so tight, Grandpa had built the newer part of the house, the main house, and connected it to the older part via a small utility room where the washing machine and dryer were kept, along with storage space.

A heavy metal door separated the laundry room from the older part of the house. I've been told that when I was a baby, we lived in the older part for a while, perhaps a year, but I was far too young to remember that period of time at all.

I walked toward the older part now, reaching for the metal door as goosebumps broke out along my arms. I didn't like the utility room. Something about it had always seemed wrong to me, off somehow.

It seemed a place where you could get trapped, a portal between the world of the older house and the new, where if you weren't careful. you might turn around and find that you weren't in the comfort of a familiar house at all, but in a small room adrift, alone, in the darkness of some alternate reality.

The door stuck briefly when I pushed against it, its bottom catching along the carpet as I forced it forward. It was lighter in this end of the house, for the huge floor-to-ceiling windows along the front wall had never been obscured with any kind of coverings, and the outdoor lights shone brightly into the room.

This part of the house, too, seemed to have not been touched since the day I last saw it.

The old upright piano sat, unused for as long as I could remember, against one wall.

Half a dozen curio cabinets stood around the room, each filled with finely crafted bird figurines. The ancient refrigerator in the small kitchen hummed quietly.

I opened the door to the small bedrooms and the bathroom. Everything was exactly the same, down to the olive-green bedspread on the bed I'd shared with my brother when we came to visit as very young children, four or five perhaps.

A sinking feeling dropped into my stomach as yet another unpleasant memory rose to the surface. We'd been asleep, my brother and I, in that very bed, when I'd woken one night to the thump of my favorite doll dropping from my hand onto the floor.

By the dim light of the neighboring bathroom, I'd seen the lumpy outline of the doll and reached toward it, but I'd quickly pulled my hand back as something large and fast moved out of the shadows.

It was the largest spider I'd ever seen, and it sat there, in the strip of light coming through the doorway, like it was waiting for me to reach down again so that it could pounce.

I'd quickly shaken my brother awake and showed him the terrifying creature lying in wait for us.

Being older, perhaps a little wiser, and certainly much braver than me, he'd taken a flying leap off the bed and made a run for the other bedroom where our mother slept.

I sat, grasping the footboard of the bed, eyes trained on that bulbous shadow on the floor, terrified that its many legs would hurtle suddenly toward me, until my mother came into the room, my brother behind her, and flipped on the light.

My mother's reaction told me that I was right to be afraid, because the spider was a tarantula, large and hairy. Instructing me not to move and pushing my brother out behind her, she disappeared for a moment and came back with a large glass bowl.

Inching tentatively forward, she swooped down with the bowl and trapped the spider beneath it.

We all took a deeply relieved breath at that point. She had then piled several heavy books on top of the bowl, then picked me up off the bed and carried me to the living room, where she did the amazing trick of pulling the couch out into a bed and making a new spot for my brother and I to sleep for the rest of the night.

The door to the room with the spider was resolutely closed and a blanket laid down across the gap at the bottom, just in case.

The next morning, over breakfast, my mother told my grandfather about the spider. He went to take care of it, a bright pink fly swatter his only weapon, returning a few minutes later and taking the fly swatter to the sink to wash it off.

I tried not to think too much about what exactly he had used it for.

A huge roll of thunder shook the house around me as I stood in the bedroom doorway, lost in memory. I jumped a little, then, holding my breath, dropped down onto my hands and knees and peered under the bed.

No spiders. Of course not.

Although we *were* out in the country. There were probably untold creatures scurrying about and hiding in the dark recesses of the house. But I didn't want to think about that.

I returned to the main house, nearly tripping over my bag, still sitting where I'd dropped it in the entry. I looked back and forth from one end of the house to the other.

Five bedrooms in the house and the thought of sleeping in any one of them made my stomach twist. I shook my head to dislodge the uneasiness building in my mind. This was Grandpa's house, the safe house of my dreams.

So why did I feel so unsettled here?

Deciding against all five bedrooms, I returned to the living room and eyed the couch. Same old couch. Brown and yellow, velvety soft to the touch but with threadbare places now that hadn't been there all those years ago.

I dropped into one of the leather armchairs that sat near the couch and rested my head in my hands. I leaned back in the chair; the leather, unused for decades perhaps, creaked in protest against my movements and sent out a cloud of fragrance that made me gasp.

It was a mixture of pipe smoke and Old Spice cologne, my grandfather's scent, and it washed over me in waves, familiar and comforting at first, then stronger until it seemed almost suffocating, a nearly tangible cloud of odor trapping me in the chair.

I shot up and stumbled a few steps away. The chair sat, silent and unmoving, innocuous.

The fragrance faded, faded, and was gone. I let out a laugh which echoed in the silence. *Better get a hold of yourself, girl. You're going wonky in this house.*

I had just turned toward the hallway, wondering where I might find spare blankets for a night on the couch, when a peal of thunder crashed sharply through the house, and every light I'd turned on went out.

A flash of lightning illuminated the room briefly, leaving floating bits of light in my eyes against the darkness. More thunder rumbled, and rain hit the windows so suddenly and loudly, like a handful of pebbles thrown against the glass, that I jumped backward, heart pounding.

After a moment to calm myself, I walked to the windows and pulled back the drapes.

Everything was black beyond the glass, not a single light to be seen. Lightning flashed again, and in the brief glow I saw rain falling hard and fast, a thick curtain of water obscuring the world beyond.

In successive flashes, I saw the poplar trees whipping and bending in a wind that seemed to come from every direction at once, sometimes throwing the rain against the window in front of me and sometimes rattling it against windows on the other side of the house.

I hoped the electricity would come back on after a moment, but the house remained dark. I pondered if the storm had simply caused a surge which flipped the breaker, or if the power was truly out until someone from the electric company came and got it working again.

I decided it couldn't hurt to check the breaker box, then wracked my brain for any idea of where it was.

Breaker boxes are not something you pay much attention to as a child, so I didn't remember its location, but an uncomfortable feeling in my stomach told me that logically it was probably in the utility room, that no-man's-land between the old house and the new.

I pulled out my phone and turned on its flashlight. A cone of light shone out in front of me, illuminating small sections of the living room as I swept it slowly back and forth.

I took a deep breath and started forward. Just as my feet stepped from the carpeted floor of the living room to the tile of the entry hall, I heard it.

Just above the noise of the rain, in a lull between the near-continuous rolls of thunder, the sound of something moving.

My brain cast around for reference and landed on the noise of cardboard boxes sliding along the ground. I swung my phone around quickly, right and left, spinning in a circle to look behind me. Only the dark and empty house greeted me, nothing moving, nothing out of place.

The sound came again, and dread rose up in my body, a tidal wave of raw nerves, and I fought against the inexplicable urge to scream, as I remembered the one place I'd seen cardboard boxes stacked up, the one place I needed to get to right now to check the breakers but the one place I suddenly absolutely did not want to go: the utility room.

I pointed my phone's light down the long, windowless hallway toward the room at the end. The light faded halfway along the hall, leaving the dreaded room in darkness.

A fear which I could not explain washed through me, a feeling like acid in my veins, a sharp pulsing in frenzied bursts just behind my eyes.

I fought for breath as a primal memory of terror reared up in my mind, flashes of recollection: myself as a child, standing in this very hallway, clutching my brother's hand as we looked down toward the utility room.

We'd seen something there, hadn't we? Seen something more than once which the adults would not believe, seen something they told us was only our imagination or a bad dream, seen something they swore could not be real but which had stopped us in our tracks and made us dread that small, unassuming room, that liminal space between the old house and the new.

I shivered, freezing and frightened, and took two or three tentative steps down the hall, the need to know just winning over the fear, keeping my light trained on that darkened space ahead.

Lightning flashed suddenly, three, four, five bolts in a row, lighting the entire house in a cold white glow, the long dark hallway ahead of me telescoping my vision toward the room at the end, where the lightning illuminated, in jerky stop-motion movements, a small, dark shape that ran from one side of the doorway, stopped in the middle for a moment, yellow eyes glowing in the darkness as it looked at me, then bolted for the other side of the room and passing beyond my sight.

I remembered then, remembered all the things about this house which had frightened me, each happy golden memory stained by one much darker, memories of noises in the night and the feeling of being watched, memories of strange handprints on the windows and the eerie sounds that my mother said were just the wind, memories of this creature, this dark silhouette at the end of the hall which my brother and I had seen all too clearly in the early morning or late evening light when the adults were crowded around the living room laughing or sleeping soundly in their beds.

In my mind's eye the image, long buried, flashed before me: a small humanoid creature, its skin a muddy green-brown, only a foot tall, with long skinny arms and legs and a distended stomach and knobby little head, with sharp, tiny teeth, and eyes that glowed a murky yellow when the light caught them.

A creature which lived somewhere in the dark corner of the utility room, or perhaps in some strange netherworld beyond which used this in-between room as a passageway.

We had seen it countless times, so many times that we had given up trying to convince our parents and grandparents and simply relied on each other's presence to tamp down the fear.

Always, always it had been in that room, and always it had stopped to glare malevolently at us, flashing those sharp teeth in a wicked smile before it ran to the other side of the room and disappeared.

I froze there in the hallway. A darkness that had nothing to do with the storm threatened to overtake me. My knees locked, the hand holding the phone light shaking uncontrollably, and I swayed where I stood.

A sound which was part scream, part sob, part wild laughter exploded from my lips, and I clamped my hand over my mouth, breathing hard against my sweaty palm.

A volley of rain slammed against the windows and then a sudden crash sounded from the utility room.

Without warning, the lights buzzed to life, my eyes blinking furiously against the sudden brightness.

At the end of the hall, beyond the doorway to the utility room, I could see a pile of boxes had fallen over, their contents spilled across the tiles.

A small ball rolled in a lazy circle and came to a stop just inside the room.

A small, brown arm shot out and grabbed it.

I screamed then.

I screamed loud and long and high, and I continued screaming as I turned and ran.

I snatched my bag from the entryway floor, wrenched the front door open, and ran out into the pouring rain and the thunder, slamming the door shut behind me.

I was soaked through in the few moments it took me to get to my car and fumble the keys from my pocket.

Inside, I threw my bag in the backseat, locked the doors, and drove all the way into the nearest town, where I checked into a tiny motel room with a saggy mattress and lumpy pillows.

No matter. I didn't sleep that night anyway.

The next morning, I called the lawyer and made it clear that I didn't want the house. He agreed graciously to take care of selling the property, likely taking my overemotional state as something due to grief rather than terror.

Then I called my brother and told him that we'd be selling the house. I left no room for argument, though he agreed readily enough.

And then I bought myself a large coffee and pulled onto the highway, headed home, desperate for sleep but knowing I wouldn't rest until I was in my own bed, safe in my own house, probably fighting my way through nightmares like I had as a child, only this time… this time my grandfather's house would no longer be the safe place my subconscious had tried to make it seem all those years ago.

This time the repressed horrors would come and… no, I shook my head. I wouldn't think like that, couldn't think like that. I wouldn't think about that thing, that impossible thing. I just wouldn't.

I rolled my window down and let the cold November air blow through the car, turned up the radio to blast over the sound of the wind, and headed home.

I'd gone thirty years since the last time I visited my grandfather's house.

And now I knew why, the real reason why, and I wondered if I'd ever truly feel safe again.

PLAYMATE

September 1918

Violet Beaumont waited patiently near the apple tree in the back garden of 16 Harrow Lane. A glorious, long, sunny September afternoon stretched out before her, hours of unencumbered leisure time, and she knew exactly how she'd be spending them.

For most of Violet's nine years of life, she'd been left to her own devices, shooed out of doors while her father saw to his patients in the front rooms of the house.

All that had changed a few weeks ago when a commotion in the garden next door caught Violet's attention. She had scaled the apple tree in a matter of moments, covering her skirts in streaks of dirt and tearing holes in her stockings.

The little care she would have given for this dishevelment disappeared entirely when she saw what was happening one house over.

For as long as Violet could remember, the neighboring house had stood empty. Not anymore.

Men in brown uniforms carried furniture and chests into the house, front and back. An enormous piano was being hauled, with much difficulty, up the garden path and through the wide-flung doors at the back of the house; this was the source of the noise which had drawn Violet's attention.

The movers were an exciting enough prospect, but what made little Violet's heart leap for joy was the sight of a girl, much the same age as herself, being bustled along by a harried young nurse.

Violet listened as the nurse told the girl to keep herself busy and out of the way, that the last thing the working men needed was a child underfoot.

The girl had brown hair that shone copper in the sun. Violet pulled out a strand of her own coal-back curls and examined it as she waited for her moment. She did not need to wait long; within minutes the movers had shoved the piano into the house, and the girl next door sat alone, sighing and bored.

Violet had crept out along one of the branches which overhung the back corner of the neighbor's garden, then dropped straight down to the ground below, landing expertly on the soles of her patent-leather shoes.

The girl jumped and let out a small shriek. She stared at Violet for a moment, eyes wide, and then both girls erupted into fits of laughter.

It was at this point that Violet knew she had found a best friend.

So, for the past several seeks Violet and her new friend, Ginny, had become bosom companions.

They each had tutors who came to drill them on spelling words and math equations and geography facts in the mornings, followed by lunch, and Ginny had an intolerable hour of piano lessons after that, but each afternoon, around two o'clock, the girls were set free to laugh and play and imagine and discover.

Rather than go in and out the front door – which might have disturbed Dr. Beaumont's patients – the girls had taken to clambering back and forth over the fence which separated their gardens, by way of the ancient, overhanging apple tree.

So.

Violet Beaumont waited patiently.

Her small mouth turned up in an excited grin when she heard the noise which meant that Ginny had finally been set loose from her obligations.

The sound was a loud, low one which echoed deeply – Ginny had hung her head down into the dark dankness of her family's rain barrel and let out a sort of ghostly whoop.

This was one of their two secret sounds: a high-pitched call meant that Violet should climb over, while the deeper one was to warn her that Ginny was coming to her side.

The girls played as the long hours of afternoon stretched toward evening, first in Violet's garden, where their dolls acted out a rather raucous tea party, then they climbed over into Ginny's yard and took turns sliding down the steep incline of her cellar door.

This last was a rewarding game right up until the first errant splinter found its home in Violet's backside; the climb back over the fence at the end of the day was unpleasant.

September stretched toward its end.. The days grew cooler, the sunlight hours shorter. Violet and Ginny were forced to condense their games, and often left off in the middle of one, promising to pick up the next day when the sun was shining again.

As the late-summer sun faded and the leaves of the apple tree turned from glossy green to dusty orange, a change took place in the city of Boston. A sickness swept the city, a new strain of flu that struck fast and hard.

Violet's father, Dr. Beaumont, was kept busier than ever, called out on visits to patients too sick to leave their own homes.

October 1918

Violet Beaumont waited patiently near the apple tree in the back garden.

Ginny had been called in early the day before when a persistent dry cough had worried her nurse.

Violet had played alone for another hour in the darkening garden before sighing and returning to the stuffy rooms of her home.

Violet stood, shifting from foot to foot in impatience; after an hour she took to chewing her fingernails nervously while she sat, her back against the apple tree, as her mind fell into worrying concern for her friend.

Ginny did not come that day.

Or the next, or the next.

A week passed before Violet saw her friend again. At the sound of movement in the next-door garden, Violet scrambled up the apple tree and peeked over the fence.

Ginny's nurse struggled to back a wheeled chair across the cobblestones of the small courtyard, finally parking it in a sunny spot.

She tucked blankets in around two small, thin legs, knelt and spoke in a quiet voice to the person in the chair, and then went back inside.

Sure that the coast was clear, Violet dropped silently from her perch and crept quietly, cautiously toward the chair.

She gasped and stepped back, one hand to her mouth, at the sight that greeted her there.

It was Ginny, but she was changed, changed so drastically in such a short time that Violet felt herself dizzy at the thought.

Ginny's skin was pale, her lips tinged with blue. Dark circles spread beneath her once-bright eyes. Her copper-chestnut hair hung lank and straight around her face; her hands, skeleton-thin, grasped each other atop the thick blanket in her lap.

"Ginny?" Violet whispered, a horrifying realization dawning in her innocent young mind.

Ginny's eyes moved slowly toward Violet, focusing at last on her friend's face. Ginny's mouth opened, but no words spilled out, only a loud cough which seemed to knock Violet back with its force.

Violet reached a hand toward her friend, in concern and sympathy, but she jerked it back quickly at the shout behind her. Ginny's nurse came running, black boot heels clunking on the stones, shooing Violet away with frantic hands.

"Go home, Violet, straight home. And don't come back," the nurse panted.

Violet started to speak, but no sound came out. She stared for a moment at the pitiful and faded countenance of her best friend, then turned and ran, scrambling up the fence, across the branches of the apple tree, down into her own yard, into the house and up the stairs to her own room, where she flung herself down on the bed and sobbed.

Days passed.

October was nothing but cold air and brisk winds. Violet was kept indoors at all times, lest she be exposed to the germs which seemed to fill the whole of the city.

She tried to ask her own nurse, the maid, and the cook about Ginny; the women only looked at her with expressions both harried and tragic and shushed her.

She barely saw her father.

She did not see Ginny at all.

Violet climbed into bed. The weather had turned cold and she was thankful for her warm blankets and the blaze which burned steadily in her small bedroom fireplace.

Her nurse tucked her in and left the room, skirts sweeping through the door behind her.

Violet lay alone in the firelit room for a long while. She found it hard to fall asleep these days, often staring at the shadows of the wind-tossed trees for hours before succumbing to slumber.

Tonight was no different.

Violet woke in the dark. The fire had burned down to smoldering embers. She lay still for a moment, fighting against the pull of sleep. She had heard something. She knew she had.

She heard it again.

A long, low sound, barely distinguishable from the moaning of the wind: a deep, ghostly, resounding whoop.

Ginny was at the rain barrel.

She was calling to Violet.

Violet jumped from her bed. She threw open her bedroom door and raced through the quiet house, meeting no one as she ran. She fought with the locks but won, flinging open the back door and rushing out into the night.

The frost-covered ground burned against the tender flesh of her bare soles; the wind passed through her nightgown as if it were nothing and made her hair fly wild around her face.

Violet did not care. Her eyes were trained on the apple tree, watching, waiting.

Ginny's form was a pale light against the darkness of the night. She scrambled down the apple trunk and came quickly to her friend, taking her by the hands.

Violet shivered, freezing and fearful, horrified and heartbroken.

Ginny shimmered in the night.

Violet, listen. Ginny's voice was a whisper, a hushed murmur against Violet's ear.

I'm sorry, Violet.

A sob rose in Violet's throat.

I'm sorry I can't play anymore.

You were my best friend, Violet. Thank you for that. We'll be friends forever, Violet, even though I'm...

The last word was too much.

Violet let out a wail, a childish sound of innocent and unrestrained anguish.

The door slammed open, hitting the back wall of the house with a crash. Violet glanced back. Her father ran toward her, fighting against the wind that filled the small garden.

He scooped the small girl up and rushed back inside.

Violet buried her face against her father's chest, his arms tight around her, the solid strength of him a welcome safety.

She stole one glance out the back door before it was pulled closed.

There was no one in the garden.

The next morning, it was discovered that the early winter storm which swept the city had caused considerable damage. The long, low branch of the apple tree in Violet's back garden, the branch which had stretched over the fence into the neighboring yard, was found cracked down the middle, lying on the snow-covered ground.

That same snow still covered the ground when Ginny's small coffin was lowered into the cemetery grounds two days later.

Violet Beaumont grew into a beautiful young woman. She was courted by many, married to one.

As the years passed, she birthed two children: a boy named Victor, and a little girl with chestnut-copper hair called Ginny.

Those children grew up and bore children of their own, and then those children did the same.

Years passed.

People lived.

People died.

October 1999

Violet Garmin, née Beaumont, waited patiently near the apple tree in the back garden.

For ninety years she had lived in the house at 16 Harrow Lane.

She was tired.

Her sweet Samuel had been gone for years. Her children, grandchildren, and great-grandchildren were happy and healthy and successful; they didn't need her anymore.

The sun dropped below the horizon.

A gentle breeze rustled the leaves of the ancient tree. From over the wall, from the neighboring yard beyond, came a sound like a ghostly moan, circling echoes in an old rain barrel.

Violet's face lifted to the branches overhead. Her faded eyes lit up; a smile tightened her soft cheeks.

A girlish giggle danced around the garden; the leaves overhead shook wildly.

Violet stood. Goosebumps prickled her body. Her legs shook, faltered, folded.

She dropped slowly, gently, to the frosted ground beneath her.

Violet stretched out an old and wrinkled hand.

Small, warm fingers wrapped around hers.

A pale glow lit the garden as the old woman laid her head down and exhaled a final breath.

The glow brightened, and in its light the silhouettes of two young girls skipped happily away, hands gripped tight together.

Friends forever.

Girl's Best Friend

It was Friday afternoon, and Ashley Lynch was preparing for a party.

She had spent the last two weeks dreaming and planning. Her sixteenth birthday was the following Tuesday, and she had invited her five best friends in the whole wide world to come spend the weekend at her family's farm.

Ashley and her mother, Patricia, had just returned from a trip into town, where they had loaded up on all the essentials required for a perfect celebration.

They entered the kitchen huffing and puffing, their arms laden with bags of soda, chips, candy, ice cream, and every kind of unhealthy junk food they could find.

Ashley's dog, Saint, danced between their legs, one-hundred-fifty pounds of fur and slobber, so excited about the humans' return that he nearly sent them both sprawling across the floor.

Finally, with their burdens deposited on the kitchen island, Patricia shooed her daughter and the drooling beast out of the room with instructions to check the rest of the house to make sure everything was ready before the guests arrived.

Ashley rolled her eyes – of course everything was ready, she'd been busy since she woke up that morning – but she gladly left the unpacking of the food to her mother and made her way upstairs to primp a little before her friends arrived.

Saint followed dutifully along and settled himself at his mistress's feet, panting happily as she touched up her mascara and tried out different hairstyles.

At seven o'clock on the dot, the doorbell rang at the Lynch farmhouse, and Ashley rushed down the stairs to answer it.

She yanked the door open. Her five friends exploded into the entry hall, shrieking and laughing, overnight bags and bedrolls in hands, ready to kick off the summer and celebrate their friend's birthday.

Saint bounded into the mix, knocking the girls aside like human bowling pins, until they all collapsed into one giant giggling mess on the stone floor.

Ashley had the whole weekend planned out, and she wasted no time in getting to it. She instructed the girls to drop their bedrolls off in the back mudroom and their bags in her bedroom.

The thunderous noise of half a dozen pairs of feet – plus four dog paws – going up and down the stairs shook the entire house, and Ashley's mother smiled and shook her head before retreating to the relative calm of her bedroom.

As the sun set below the western horizon, Ashley ushered her friends outside. There, on the huge sandstone patio, they spread their sleeping bags out and arranged chairs around the firepit set into the ground.

Saint sniffed at the sleeping bags until finding the one that smelled like his owner.

He turned three times in a circle, let out one chuffing sneeze, and settled himself down, his head on his paws and his eyes alert and watching from underneath his shaggy fur.

The other girls shrieked as Ashley started a fire in the pit. She rolled her eyes at their silly city-girl ways. Ashley herself had grown up out here on the farm, riding horses and chasing pigs, hands in the dirt from sunup till sundown, planting, weeding, harvesting.

She'd spent countless days swimming in the creek out past the South Field and almost as many nights sleeping under the stars as under a roof.

Ashley showed her friends how to roast hot dogs over the fire and then slide them off the end of their sticks directly into a waiting bun.

When they had eaten their fill of hot dogs, she took out graham crackers, marshmallows, and chocolate bars and showed them how to make s'mores.

It didn't take long at all for the girls' faces to be covered in melty chocolate and graham cracker crumbs stuck in bits of gooey marshmallow.

Saint happily padded over and helped out by licking each of the girls in turn, making some of them shriek and some of them gag. Ashley simply laughed and called Saint to her, bribing him away from her friends with the few leftover hot dogs.

The girls sat around the fire for hours, talking and laughing, sharing the latest gossip and teasing each other about the boys they were currently in love with.

Having been apart for two whole weeks since school let out, they had lots to discuss.

Eventually the loud conversation died down to quiet whispers.

Above them the great expanse of the sky stretched as far as the eye could see, a thousand pinprick stars twinkling down at them.

One by one, as the hour approached midnight, the girls began to yawn.

Even Saint, who had curled up next to Ashley's chair, occasionally raising his head to lick lovingly at her hand, was now sound asleep and snoring.

"I think it must be time to bed down for the night," Ashley announced quietly, standing up and stretching her arms over her head and then bending down to touch her toes.

Saint stirred and lifted his head to watch her.

The fire had burned down to embers by then, and Ashley poured a couple of bottles of water over the remaining logs, causing a quiet sizzle and a thin plume of smoke which rose into the air and disappeared into the darkness.

The girls tramped slowly inside and up the stairs, changing into their pajamas and brushing their teeth.

Back outside, they adjusted their sleeping bags until they were arranged in a circle, with their heads pointed in toward the center so they could continue talking as they lay there.

Ashley climbed into her own bag and snuggled down into its warmth. Though it was nearly summer, the nights out here in the middle of nowhere could get chilly, and she was thankful for Saint's warmth as he settled in beside her.

She was happy with the way the party was going so far. Just catching up had been fun, but she had lots of things planned for the next day. She went over the itinerary in her head as the other girls murmured softly to each other.

"Ew, Ashley, that's kind of gross," Beth's voice brought her out of her own thoughts and back to the moment.

Ashley raised her head to look at the girl next to her.

"What's gross?" she asked, brow furrowed.

"Uh, your dog is gross." Beth gave a sleepy giggle.

"Does he always do that?"

Ashley followed Beth's eyes and realized that she was watching Saint lick her hand. She gave a little chuckle.

"I guess it might seem kind of gross to you guys, but I don't mind. It's just something we've done since I was little. It makes me feel safe."

Beth propped herself up on her elbows and gave Ashley an incredulous look.

"Dog spit makes you feel safe?"

Some of the other girls giggled.

"Yep," Ashley answered, raising her hand to stroke Saint's soft fur before dropping it back down again.

He promptly licked her fingers.

"When I was a little girl, I would sometimes get scared of things – you know, monsters, bogeymen, something in the closet. But Saint sometimes slept in my room, on the floor next to my bed, and when he was there, I felt safe.

"I was so afraid sometimes that I didn't dare open my eyes, afraid of what monsters I would see, so I would call Saint's name and he would come into my room and lay there and lick my hand.

"I didn't have to open my eyes to know that he was there. Eventually he spent every night in my room, and even today, though I'm not scared of little kid stuff anymore, if I have a nightmare or something, I'll wake up and feel him licking my hand and know that everything is OK."

The other girls seemed to consider this. If any of them thought it strange, they didn't say so.

Quiet conversation continued for a few more minutes but was quickly replaced by slow breathing and soft snores.

Ashley burrowed down into her sleeping bag once more. She closed her eyes and let out a contented sigh. Saint's tongue stroked against her fingers once, twice, the feeling familiar and comforting, and then she was asleep.

The rising sun the next morning elicited groans from six forms hunkered down inside sleeping bags. It was hard to sleep late when you slept outside, and before long the girls were sitting up, rubbing the sleep from their eyes, and stretching.

Saint stood up, did his own stretch, shook his shaggy coat and licked Ashley's face as she squinted in the brightness.

It took some urging – and some teasing and a little bit of threatening – on Ashley's part to get everyone up and moving, but within an hour they had rolled up their bags, gotten dressed, and had breakfast.

Ashley's announcement that they were going horseback riding was met with a mixture of excitement and dread. Some of her friends had never been near a horse, much less ridden one, but she assured them that she would show them how to do it and that their family horses were as gentle and tame as could be.

Mid-morning found the girls riding the many trails which crisscrossed the Lynch family's land.

The crops were flourishing but still small, and the views across the hilly countryside were beautiful.

Even Beth and Lyla – the girls who had been the most nervous about riding – got the hang of it and were able to relax and enjoy the scenery.

They talked as they rode, laughing as teenage girls do, discussing the boys they knew, teasing one another about not-so-secret crushes.

Ashley was riding with her head turned back to give her opinion on the boy of the moment when Chelsea interrupted her.

"What's that up there, Ash?" she asked, and Ashley faced forward to follow the line of sight from Chelsea's outstretched finger.

There was something ahead on the path, but she couldn't be sure what it was until she rode a little closer.

Ashley pulled her horse to a standstill and the others did the same. She gazed down at the object on the ground next to her. She tilted her head one way and then the other trying to make sense of it.

"What is it?" All the girls were curious.

"It's a shoe. Like, a house shoe – a slipper," Ashley answered.

They all agreed that this was strange, especially since the Lynch land was clearly marked as private property with *No Trespassing* signs posted every sixty feet along the perimeter fence.

Ashley shielded her eyes with her hand and gazed up at the blue sky above them.

"I guess, maybe, a bird dropped it here?"

The idea seemed plausible enough to her friends, but Ashley continued to think about the slipper's strange appearance as they clicked their tongues at their horses and continued along the trails toward home.

Ashley's parents met them at the barn and took over the job of caring for and putting away the horses.

Saint came bounding up the walk as soon as they neared the house and followed the girls inside as they descended ravenously upon the kitchen.

After a lunch of sandwiches and a little time to rest, Ashley instructed them all to change into their swimsuits, grab a towel, and meet her on the back patio.

She then led them down the short walk past the barn, through a screen of trees, and around the side of the South Field to the creek.

The girls shouted in delight as they waded in; at its deepest the creek came to their shoulders.

They spent several hours wading, swimming, and splashing each other, thankful for the creek's cool water as the sun shone down hot and the temperature of the June day rose past ninety degrees.

Saint jumped in once, soaking himself to the skin. He paddled around for five minutes and then climbed back up the bank, shaking himself so furiously that the water sprinkled the shrieking girls like a cold shower.

He then settled himself in a sunny spot nearby and napped through the remainder of the afternoon.

Only once did he raise his head and growl in the general direction of the wooded area that bordered the creek; Ashley assured the girls there was nothing to worry about, either he had been dreaming or had picked up the scent of some small animal in the underbrush.

When the shadows of the trees around the creek began to stretch long across the ground, Ashley announced that it was time to head back to the house.

The girls climbed up out of the creek and took to rubbing themselves down with their towels, squeezing the dripping water from their hair and wiping sandy grit from the bottoms of their feet.

With their towels wrapped around them, they began the walk back to the house.

"What time is it, anyway?" Miranda asked, walking backward along the trail to address the others.

"Yeah," Tessa added, "I'm starving. I hope it's dinnertime."

Ashley glanced down at her wrist to check the time, then stopped and swore under her breath.

"You guys go on. I took my watch off so it wouldn't get wet, and I forgot to put it back on."

Ashley turned back as the others walked on, and Saint, loyal to his mistress, trotted along beside her as she made her way back to the creek bed.

She scanned the area where they had kicked off their shoes and laid their towels. The bright pink of her watch band should have been easy to see, but she couldn't spot it.

She moved closer to the trees and weedy growth, further into the shadows, moving thorny branches aside as her eyes scanned the ground.

A sound made her look up, a rustle in the brambles further down the creek. Her eyes caught movement, tall grasses swaying and branches settling back as if something had just pushed through them.

Saint gave two warning barks.

Ashley stood perfectly still, eyes scanning the area. There was no more movement, no more sound. A cold feeling crept up her spine and she shivered as goosebumps broke out along her arms.

Turning around, her eyes fell on a flash of pink on the sandy shore of the creek. Her watch.

She was sure it hadn't been there, right in plain sight, just a minute before. She pushed her way out of the undergrowth and picked up the watch.

She gave the area one last glance before hurrying away, up the path toward the house to catch up with her friends, Saint following behind her.

Ashley chose not to tell the other girls about her strange encounter. As jumpy as they all were, the story would frighten them and then she'd have a bunch of whiny scaredy-cats to deal with all night long.

After they were dried and dressed again, they settled in the large family room with three pizzas and the big-screen TV.

They spent half an hour looking through movies on Netflix before finally deciding on a cheesy-looking old slasher flick.

After the slasher was over, Ashley headed to the kitchen to make some popcorn before they started the next movie.

While she waited for the kernels to pop in the microwave, she pulled out her phone and checked her social media feeds.

Her forehead furrowed in concern as she scanned the news headlines for her area. The top story, the one that everyone was talking about, posting about, sharing, and retweeting was about the escape of a patient from a high-security mental institution about fifty miles away.

Ashley considered passing on this information to her friends, but once again decided she didn't want to scare them.

After another campy movie, the girls' eyes were beginning to feel heavy. A long day of horseback riding and swimming had brought them all to a comfortable level of exhaustion, and just after eleven o'clock, they put on their pajamas, crawled back into their sleeping bags, and began the process of settling in for the night.

Ashley was the last one to fall asleep.

She would start to doze, and then her mind would flash with the memory of that strange slipper on the trail, or the movement in the bushes near the creek.

She thought of the news about the escaped mental patient, and about the scary-not-scary horror movies they'd watched.

She told herself that they were fifty miles from the psychiatric hospital and there was no way the guy could have made it to their farm that quickly.

She told herself that her daddy had a whole arsenal of guns, and there were six of them out here on the patio, six against one.

She told herself that she was being silly and paranoid. She told herself all kinds of things which were meant to be comforting, but only one of them brought her any real comfort: that Saint was there, and he would protect her.

She scooted herself and her sleeping bag a few inches over, so that Saint's massive body was right against hers.

She stroked his head a few times, then let her hand drop.

Saint's warm, wet tongue lapped against the skin of her palm, and the old feeling of safety washed over her, and she slept.

The man watched from a distance. He had been watching them, the pretty girls with their pretty laughs and their pretty hair and their pretty necks, since the night before.

Now, under the cover of darkness, with the sound of his movements masked by the wind in the trees and the cricket-song, he crept forward, toward the place where six teenage girls slept soundly, tired out by their long day.

A glint of silver, moonlight on metal, flashed in the darkness.

Ashley slept surprisingly well that night. A few times she half-roused at some slight noise or a bit of wind that lifted the hair of her scalp.

Once she thought it might have started raining as a few warm drops hit her outstretched hand.

She never rose fully to wakefulness.

Every time she stirred, Saint's tongue would lap against her hand four or five times until her breathing returned to its sleep-slowed rhythm.

When Ashley did wake, it was with a jolt. She sat straight up, eyes wide, at the sound of a woman's scream.

She looked around wildly, and her eyes met those of her mother standing just outside the patio doors.

For a moment, Ashley didn't understand why her mother was screaming. For a moment she thought she must still be dreaming.

Then her eyes fell on the circle of her friends in their sleeping bags: on their perfectly still bodies, on the blood that surrounded them.

Ashley's mother came running, stumbling across the patio, trying not to step in the pooling blood as she made her way to her.

Patricia fell to her knees beside Ashley's sleeping bag and wrapped her daughter in her arms.

Ashley's eyes darted from one bloody sleeping bag to the next, until finally they came to rest on the mass of bloody fur right next to her.

It was then that she, too, began to scream.

It took twenty minutes for the police to arrive, driving all the way from town out to the Lynch farm.

It took two paramedics to carefully, gently, extract Ashley from her sleeping bag and check her over.

Aside from shock, she was completely unharmed. A few drops of blood had dried along one hand and arm, but the blood was not her own.

The police officers gathered the family together in the living room as a forensics team went over the patio and people from the coroner's office began bagging and removing the bodies one by one.

There were questions that had no good answers: had they seen anything suspicious, heard anything, noticed anything out of the ordinary?

Ashley's parents stared at their daughter in disbelief as she recounted the odd slipper on the trail, the mysterious movement in the underbrush.

Why, they wanted to know, hadn't she told them about these things?

All Ashley could do was shrug and cry as she told them that she hadn't wanted to ruin her weekend with her friends.

The grim-faced detectives finished their initial questioning and told the family to sit tight.

As they stood to go, Ashley blurted out, "I just don't understand, though."

One of the detectives, a woman with a motherly look about her, knelt in front of Ashley.

"What don't you understand?" she asked.

Ashley looked her in the eyes and spoke through her sobs.

"I don't understand why Saint didn't protect us. I always knew he would protect me, always. But he didn't. I don't understand it."

"Well," the woman said, and her eyes flicked up toward Ashley's parents as if looking for permission to say the next words, "We think — we think that the killer probably slit Saint's throat first, so that he wouldn't bark and wake the girls up."

Ashley stared at her hands, considering this for a moment.

Then she looked up.

"No," she said. "No, because Saint licked my hand all night long. That's what he does, see, what we do, what we've always done. He sleeps next to me and licks my hand when bad dreams make me restless.

"And he did it last night. I remember it. I remember him licking my hand all night long."

The detective looked intently into Ashley's face for a moment before opening her mouth to speak.

Before she could get a word out, one of the officers working outside came to the patio door and spoke.

"You guys might want to see this."

The detectives exchanged a glance and then headed toward the patio. Ashley and her parents stood and followed them.

The five girls' bodies had been removed, their bloody sleeping bags stuffed into evidence bags, leaving five bloody stains on the sandstone.

The sun was high in the sky by this point, the day hot and humid already, and the scent of blood was overwhelming, a metallic fug that Ashley could taste in the back of her throat.

Only Ashley's sleeping bag remained, with the body of Saint lying beside it. It was around the dog's body that a small crowd of people were gathered.

One officer was crouching down next to Saint.

"Look at this," he said, and with gloved hands, he rolled the dog's body away from the sleeping bag.

Beneath him lay a piece of paper, one edge saturated with blood.

On the paper were written four words which made Ashley's entire body erupt in goosebumps.

A wave of nausea rose up inside her so quickly that she turned and vomited on the spot.

A photographer took a few pictures of the note where it lay, and then the man crouching next to it picked it up and placed it carefully into a clear plastic bag.

Ashley caught one more glance of the paper before it was whisked away, before her parents ushered her back into the house.

In childish block letters, the note read:

HUMANS CAN LICK TOO.

Crybaby Bridge

I think most places have some version of Crybaby Bridge.

The stories behind the hauntings vary slightly from place to place: a child fell in by accident and was drowned, or a mother threw her baby off the bridge to hide the fact of its birth; sometimes the mother was driving a car which somehow went off the bridge and they both drowned.

In rarer cases a man murders the mother and then throws her baby off the bridge.

Regardless of how the supposed deaths occurred, the results seem to be the same: stand on the bridge at night and you can hear the ghostly cries of the long-lost baby.

I know this story now, know that it's a widespread bit of folklore (or, perhaps, fakelore), know that it's just a spooky tale people like to tell.

But the first time I heard it – the first time I experienced it – back in 1993, at the age of twelve, well, that's a story all on its own…

Katie and I had been friends since first grade. I can remember our first-grade teacher, Mrs. Davis, introducing us and telling me that Katie was new to our school and maybe I could be her friend and show her around.

Now, this was a twisty bit of psychology on the part of Mrs. Davis (she was good at that, actually) because I was probably the shyest child in the entire school, and Katie didn't really need my help in any way.

But, Mrs. Davis, in her been-a-schoolteacher-for-decades wisdom, put us together, gave six-year-old me a job to do, made me feel both important and like maybe I wasn't the most introverted and socially awkward person in the world, and *voila*! Katie and I were friends.

Oh, there were struggles along the way. In the second grade, Katie and I were in separate classes, and she became friends with Tiffany; that was a thorn in the side of our friendship ever after. (Think Mean Girls except with elementary-age students, and you'll be able to imagine Tiffany perfectly.)

But Katie and I were friends, and Tiffany and I rubbed along as best we could.

We completed elementary school and started the awkward and painful journey that is the pre-teen years. We went to middle school where the crack between us widened, as I fell further and further into the "smart kid" chasm and Katie and Tiffany drifted into "popular kid" territory.

Still, when Katie's thirteenth birthday rolled around in October of 1993, we were all there together at the sleepover: Katie, Tiffany, Stacy (a new-ish addition to the group, she'd moved in next-door to Katie in fifth grade), and me.

Katie was turning thirteen, which was a *big deal*. She was the oldest of all of us by several months. I wouldn't hit the teen years until the next June; Stacy and Tiffany had birthdays one day apart in July.

So, thirteen, being such a *big deal*, required an awesome party. Or at least, what we thought was awesome back then.

We started out with makeovers.

That's right. Katie's mom brought in an actual Mary Kay representative to teach us how to put on make-up. (My sensitive skin would have a reaction to that brand of products, and I'd have to wash most of it back off.)

Then we went for a *professional photo shoot.* (The photographer was a friend of the family, whose four daughters went to school with us.)

After that, while we were all dressed up and made-up and hyped up, we went to the school dance.

The *school dance*.

Ugh.

It was the first school dance I ever attended, and the last. Seriously. I didn't even go to prom. I may have been traumatized by that seventh-grade dance. Oh, the awkwardness. And the fact that my friends didn't seem to have a problem with embarrassing me in front of large groups of people.

But we won't talk about that.

And now, folks, the story gets good.

We went to visit a Halloween haunted-house-display. This *was* the middle of October, after all.

I was now officially on my own turf, in many ways.

First of all, Halloween, all that spooky scary stuff: I was already deep down the horror-literature rabbit hole, even though my friends didn't know it yet. It wasn't *cool* to read as much as I did, you know, so I didn't talk about it.

But Halloween was my thing. I loved it. *And* it just so happened that I was way more in the know about this particular Halloween attraction than any of my friends had any chance of being.

Hill House.

Now, they didn't call it that. At least I don't think they did. Or if they did, I was still too young to understand the humor in it. It was, literally, the Hills' house.

The Hill family lived just down the street from me. They had three boys: Jeremy, Jason, and Justin. (Lord, save us from alliterative child naming!)

None of them were exactly my age; Justin was a few years younger, Jason and Jeremy one and three years older, respectively.

But Jeremy was one of my older brother's best friends, and we'd lived down the street from them my whole life, and so the great Hill House Halloween Spectacular (again, not its official title) was nothing new to me.

The Hills loved Halloween. At least their father did; I'm not convinced the kids cared all that much, but I never asked.

Regardless, they did Halloween in a big way at their house. And each year, they did it bigger.

What started as a small yard display had turned into an elaborate production complete with animatronics and fog machines.

The spectacle pulled in so many visitors that they opened it up for extra days. At first it was a couple of days before Halloween, then a week, then they added in every weekend in October.

Halloween night in our neighborhood was insane. Hundreds of children ringing the doorbell for hours, all coming to our street because of the Hill House just a few yards down.

I don't even want to think about how much my parents spent on candy every year.

But, anyway, it wasn't Halloween, not yet. It was Friday the 15th, and we were off to see the Hill House.

Katie's house and ours were only about three blocks apart, so we walked, us four girls and Katie's parents. I felt a strange sense of pride in the fact that we passed my house as we went, a strange glory in my connection to the Hill family, however slight it might be.

We toured the Halloween displays. I don't remember if the other girls liked them. I don't remember if they shrieked when the vampire shot up out of its coffin or if they were grossed out by the things in jars in Frankenstein's lab. I don't even remember my own reactions.

The things that happened later eclipsed the silly Halloween display.

Our fun over, we walked back to Katie's house.

It was getting late at this point, or what passes for late when you're twelve. It was probably ten o'clock, but it was pitch black outside and getting cool enough that we pulled on our jackets before we headed out to Katie's backyard to hang out.

I should have known something was up at this point.

Why on earth would a bunch of twelve and thirteen-year-old girls want to hang out in the cold and the dark outdoors instead of sitting inside, where it was warm, maybe with some snacks and a movie?

Because Katie's parents needed us out of the house for a while, that's why.

And of course, Katie needed a prime spooky atmosphere to tell us about this story she'd heard from her parents:

There's this place, not far from here, called Crybaby Bridge. It's called that because one day a baby died there, in the water, and people go out there at night and stand and listen and they say if you're very quiet, you can hear the sound of the baby crying.

I can't say what the other girls thought about this story, but I felt a little surge of excitement. I'd heard of weird, creepy, haunted places before, of course, but I had no idea there was one "not far" from where I lived.

"We should ask Mom and Dad if we can go there tonight!" Katie suggested.

This was met with a chorus of agreements.

"No, no, it's too late," said her parents.

"Awwww," we all groaned.

We hung out a while longer. I'm not a night owl, and I was getting sleepy. Katie couldn't stop bringing up the idea of Crybaby Bridge. "We'll ask again at eleven o'clock, " she said, and she kept track of time on her watch.

We counted down the last seconds like it was New Year's Eve or something.

Amazingly, at eleven o'clock exactly, Katie's parents came out into the yard. Katie begged once more for the chance to visit Crybaby Bridge.

Her parents hemmed and hawed dramatically before agreeing.

We all took a moment to absorb this unexpected acquiescence, and then we loaded up in the back of their enormous van.

Katie, Tiffany, and Stacy claimed the spots on the bench seat along the back. I got the weird sideways-facing seat next to them.

The houses we passed as we drove were decked out in fake spiderwebs and hanging sheet-ghosts and pumpkins not yet carved.

We left the city and drove down dark, quiet country roads, the van bumping along gravel and potholes as the four of us giggled nervously.

"Oh," Katie's dad called from the front seat, "You know, before we get to Crybaby Bridge, we're going to have to pass Sparky's Graveyard!"

My ears perked. Yet another place I'd never heard of.

Sparky's Graveyard, it turns out, at least as far as I can tell, is a truly local haunt. I've not found references to anything by that name in any place other than the Tulsa/Sand Springs area. Even within local stories, however, there are variations.

The location of the graveyard is debated: some say it's south of town, some west. That it's a small graveyard once tended by a man called Sparky seems to be the common thread.

Some say he was an albino with glowing red eyes. Some say the graveyard was originally an Indian burial ground and Sparky is (somehow) a headless Native American spirit. Still others say that the cemetery was created for the African American community and that Sparky was an old black man.

Whatever the original purpose of the graveyard and whoever Sparky was back when he was still among the living, the story now goes that the spirit of Sparky still roams the grounds, and that Sparky, being a cranky old man in life, is still a cranky old man in death, and that anyone who ventures into the hallowed grounds of which he is caretaker will be subject to pushes, scratches, and swatting at the hands if you dare to touch a tombstone.

"They say if you drive past at night, you can still see the light of his lantern, held high in his hand as he roams among the graves, making sure no one disturbs them. Here, we're coming up on it now—"

I turned in my seat, pressed my face to the window.

By the faint light of the moon, I could just make out the crooked stones jutting up through the earth, a graveyard overgrown with trees, more forest than anything at this point.

I narrowed my eyes, peering into the darkness.

A building - a small house, perhaps - far back among the trees. And… what was that? A light, a dim yellow light that swayed in the wind as we passed?

And then it was gone, and we were driving away down the road, and I was a little scared but excited by it, and a little sad that it was already over.

A little while later, the van slowed.

"Here we are," Katie's mother intoned.

The keys pulled from the ignition, the van went suddenly dark and silent. We sat, unmoving, as we listened, waiting for something, anything, to happen.

The silence rose up around us, pounding against my eardrums. No one spoke, we scarcely breathed.

A sound, nearby. Footsteps? A branch scraping against the top of the van? Some homicidal maniac come to murder a bunch of silly girls? We'd all heard it, we looked at each other, from one face to another, until finally someone let out a nervous giggle.

"I really thought I heard something!"

"That freaked me out!"

"What *was* that?"

"This is creepy!"

Our whispers overlapped and we all laughed at ourselves and I was laughing too until suddenly I heard the sound again and this time it was *right behind me,* and the other three girls all stopped talking, stopped laughing, and their eyes all fixed on a point just over my shoulder and I turned my head ever so slowly to see what they were looking at.

Two pale hands with long nails were scratching down the window.

Slowly, rising up from the bottom of the window until it was level with my own terrified eyes, there appeared a face – ghastly, pale, wrinkled and horrific, long tangled hair blowing in the wind.

I let out a scream and jumped out of my seat.

I was on the floor, tangled among the other girls' feet, looking up at the face in the window.

A whole chorus of shrieks and squeals erupted until we realized that Katie was laughing and then Tiffany said, "Hey, is that… my mom?"

And then the joke was over and two sets of parents – Katie's and Tiffany's – were grinning as they opened the sliding door and gestured for us all to climb out.

I didn't know whether to laugh or cry or be angry that they'd tricked us, but the other girls were back to giggling and the parents thought the whole thing was hysterical and Tiffany's mom was running her fingers through her long dark hair to get the tangles out and of course the make-up she had on was obvious and the fake nails looked ridiculous and so I shrugged to myself and went along with it all.

"Take a look around," the parents told us, and so we did.

The bridge was small, just wide enough for one car.

The wooden rails along each side were old and damp. The creek was perhaps ten feet below us, surrounded on either side by dark trees.

Looking over the edge, I could see that the water was only three or four feet deep at the deepest point. The creek was more mud than water, the ground covered with a slimy blanket of wet leaves, black in the moonlight.

There were things in the creek, up the sides of the creek bed.

Diapers.

Baby bottles.

One old-fashioned baby carriage lay on its side, rusty and half-full of water.

And though I could hear the parents saying that people must come out here and throw these things into the creek for fun or to scare other people, all I could do was look at that carriage with a sick feeling in my stomach.

Whether it was true or not that a baby had died in this creek at some point in the past didn't matter; as I looked at that carriage, one enormous wheel staring up at the sky, all I could think of was the horror that the mother must have felt and the confusion of the baby when suddenly it couldn't breathe and no one came to help it.

All I could think of was the pain and the grief and the awfulness of it all and everyone else was laughing but I didn't think it was funny in the slightest, and from out of the woods or perhaps just out of my own imagination there rose a thin, reedy cry that might have been an owl or might have been a baby, and I swear that a few bubbles rose to the top of that murky water and popped and the wind howled through the treetops and autumn leaves rushed across the path and some fell into the water and floated until they reached the gummed-up shores and came to rest.

And then far off up the road a pair of headlights crested the horizon and the parents were telling us all to get back into the van, that we'd have to get off the bridge so the other car could cross it.

We clambered back in and I sat turned toward the window, watching that baby carriage and thinking of how it would feel to have those slimy leaves all around you, inhaling their scent as you sucked the mud into your lungs; as we turned around and passed back over the bridge, in my mind's eye I could picture a baby in that carriage, swaddled in white lace, the dirty water staining the edges of the blankets as the child's lifeless eyes stared up at the moon.

We went home – or, to Katie's house, anyway – and we put on our pajamas and ate leftover cake.

I remember odd things about the night, like the fact that we had Barney plates and napkins (a joke because Katie hated Barney with a passion) and that I was wearing a dark green peasant blouse and that Stacy climbed into her sleeping bag and passed out first because she had to leave early the next morning for a softball game.

That was seventh grade.

By the time we entered high school, we weren't really friends anymore, which is to say that Katie and Tiffany were still best friends, Stacy still had her own other friends, and I found myself unhappy with the shallowness and self-absorption that so many of the girls my age displayed and set out to make a new set of friends.

The friends that saw me through the rest of high school were the super-smart kids and the creative-writing kids and the band nerds and the Stoners and my new best friend, Amanda, who I'd known since fourth grade and suddenly realized was a much more real person than any of the other girls I'd been hanging around with for my entire childhood.

Nine years later, in 2002, a freight barge floating down the Arkansas River would collide with a pier supporting the I-40 bridge near Webbers Falls, approximately seventy-five miles from where I lived.

Fourteen people were killed when the bridge collapsed.

As the news camera panned across the river, you could see items drifting along in the current or pushed up against the banks, rocking back and forth in the small waves.

Something near the shore caught my eye: a diaper floating in the water.

I had a four-month-old baby myself at the time. It made me think of that long-ago night standing on an old bridge looking down into murky water and thinking of losing your child that way.

It made me sick.

Looking back, I realize now that I started the process of learning a lot of things about myself on that night.

The fact that friends come and go, that people sometimes outgrow each other.

The fact that I felt things more deeply than many of those around me. That my imagination was both a terrible and a wondrous thing.

That there is no horror as real or as heartbreaking as the horrors we face every day, the horror of the pain we cause each other, intentionally or not; the horror of life and death and grief.

I can still see it so clearly now in my mind: the world cast in bluey-blackness, silver moonlight gilding the edges of things. Half-bare trees all around, thick mud beneath, the bridge itself barely safe enough to drive a car over.

I can feel the presence of the others standing what feels like both mere feet and many miles away, conversation muted like sounds heard underwater.

I can feel the chill, simultaneously unnerving and exciting, that raced along my spine and down my arms as I pictured in my head the horror of an imaginary death.

I guess you could say that on that October midnight in 1993, a darkness permeated my skin, skittered through my veins, sank into my bones, plunged into my pumping heart, and took up residence in my brain.

And, though it wasn't my intent when I started writing this story, I've realized something as I sit here at my laptop: on Crybaby Bridge all those years ago, the first dark, tiny, horrific story idea took root in my mind. An autumn wind whistled, a bridge creaked beneath the weight of too many people, a spectral cry sounded on the air, and a writer was born.

AUTHOR'S NOTES

VICE

There is a hint of truth in this story. The original tale is one of my grandmother's, but rather than being something which she saw happening to other people, it is the tale of something she experienced herself. Always in poor health, Grandma Nan spent a lot of time in the hospital. One night she awoke to shifting shadows and a dark creature sitting on her chest, one which she described as looking like a small but evil monkey, whose weight crushed her lungs until she thought she would surely die.

Whether she truly saw a glimpse into the world of the supernatural or was just having a drug-induced hallucination (she was likely on very strong pain meds) is up for debate. In my version of the story, I took her brief experience and tried to turn it into something even more sinister.

BURGLAR MAN

This story – which I had a lot of fun writing, by the way – is based on an old song that my grandmother used to sing. She sang it to my mother, who sang it to me, and I in turn have sung it many times to my own children. We even sang it at church camp one year, if you can believe it. You can find four different versions of the song cataloged in the Max Hunter Folk Song Collection at Missouri State University by visiting this link:

https://maxhunter.missouristate.edu/songinformation.aspx?ID=579

The version we sing in my family goes as follows:

I'll tell you a story 'bout a burglar man
Who decided to rob a house.
He opened up the window and he crept in
Just as quiet as a mouse.
And thinking of the money he'd get
As under the bed he lay,
That burglar man saw a sight that night
That made his hair turn gray!
About nine o'clock an old maid came in.
"Oh, I'm so tired!" she said.
And thinking all was well,
She forgot to look under the bed.
Well she took out her teeth and her big glass eye
And the hair right off of her head.
That burglar man had nineteen fits
Getting out from under that bed.
From under the bed that burglar came
He was a total wreck.
The old maid didn't scream at all,
She just grabbed him around the neck.
And from the drawer a revolver she drew,
And this is what she said:
"Young man, you're going to marry me
Or I'll blow off the top of your head!"
Well, he looked at her teeth and her big glass eye
And he saw no place to scoot.
He turned to the old maid standing there and said
"Lady, for the Lord's sake, shoot!"

CRIES FROM THE ATTIC

This was a story which I had forgotten until my brother mentioned it to me. The original story is simply that there was a man who killed his wife and child in the attic of their house and then as a ghost lured unsuspecting victims up to the attic by making the child cry. I added some details to flesh out the story and made the ghostly baby's cry come from the father instead, because I didn't like the idea that the innocent mother and baby ghosts would be stuck for all eternity in that attic with their tormentor. Young ghost-hunting women apparently don't merit as much sympathy with me. Sorry, Jessica.

UP ALL NIGHT

This story is based – mostly – on a real-life experience of my grandmother's. She really was a single mom raising two children, and she really did have a strange man that snuck around her house for multiple nights. The police really did say they couldn't do anything about it, they really did say she could only get away with shooting the guy if he was actively breaking in, and she really did stay up all night with a shotgun across her knees. The story is more or less true to fact right up to the point where Marla shoots a bullet straight down into the floor – my grandmother did that. In the real version of events, though, this one shot was enough to scare off the prowler to the point that he never came back. Grandma always said, though, that she'd made the plan to shoot him and drag him halfway into the window to make it look as if he were actively coming in, if that was what it took. For my story, I figured … why not let her get that vengeance? The lesson here: Hell hath no wrath like a mama whose children are threatened.

FIERY EYES AND BLOODY BONES

There's so much to sort through with this story. I did a little research and while there are plenty of references out there to Bloody Bones, and to the monstrous duo Rawhead and Bloody Bones, none of the stories quite matched up with Grandma Nan's version. These stories have been around a long time. There are similar tales found among old Scottish and Irish nursery stories, African American folk stories and tales found all throughout both the Appalachian and Ozark regions.

I wanted to tell Grandma Nan's version specifically, so I gathered up all the memories various family members had of the story; it seems that every time the story was told it was a little different, so people tended to remember different things. Common themes, however, that ran throughout were: a naughty child, an abandoned building, an old mattress and a troubled sleep. To some, the creature's *name* was Fiery Eyes and Bloody Bones, to others, these were just descriptions of the monster's appearance. The use of the phrase, "I'm on the first (second, third…) step," is something that we see a lot in stories like this. It's a technique for building tension used in this story but also in The Antique Doll, The Golden Arm, The Big Toe, The Old Panther, and various other folk tales.

Since Grandma's version was the only one I could find that made mention of fiery eyes, I wanted to make sure that the eyes played a significant part of my story, so I made them cast a firelit glow in front of the creature wherever it went.

The character of Zeke Blackwell is based loosely on a whole family of cousins I once knew (not *my* family) who all were very loud, very opinionated, and very rude. I smashed them all together into one unlikable character. I still felt a little bad for feeding him to old Fiery Eyes, though.

BLOSSOM

Blossom is the second story in this collection based on an old song. Again, my grandmother sang it, my mother sang it, and though I don't like it as much as Burglar Man, I've even been known to sing it a time or two myself. The song was obviously written to warn of the dangers of liquor consumption so when I made it into a story I wanted that same sort of in-your-face, beware-all-you-sinners type of feel, so I decided to write it up as a newspaper article obviously penned by a strict teetotaler.

The Max Hunter Folk Song Collection has three versions of this particular song, which can be found here:

https://maxhunter.missouristate.edu/songinformation.aspx?ID=1482

The version we sing in my family goes like this:

Oh dear, I'm so sad and so lonesome
And I wish that my mama would come
She told me to shut up my big brown eyes
And before I'd wake up she'd be home

She said she was going to see Grandma
Who lives by the river so bright
Well perhaps she has fallen in there
And perhaps she won't be home tonight

Well I guess I'll go out and find Papa
I suppose he has stopped at the store
'Tis a great pretty store filled with bottles
And I wish he wouldn't go there anymore

Sometimes he is sick when he comes home
And he stumbles and falls on the stair
And once when he came in the parlor
He kicked at my poor little chair

Mama was so pale and frightened
And hugged me up close to her breast
And called me her dear little Blossom
And I guess I've forgotten the rest

But I love him and I guess I'll go find him
Perhaps he'll come home with me soon
And then it won't be dark and lonely
Waiting for Mama to come

Out in the night went the baby
Her tiny heart beating with fright
Til her tired feet reached that gin palace
All radiant with music and light

The little hand pushed the door open
Though her touch was as light as a breath
And her little feet entered the portal
That leads but to ruin and to death

“Oh Papa,” she cried as she reached him
And her voice echoed out sweet and clear
“I thought if I came I would find you
And I is so glad you is here.

The lights are so pretty, dear Papa,
And I think that the music is sweet,
But I guess it’s ‘most suppertime, Papa,
For Blossom wants something to eat.”

A moment the bleared eyes gazed wildly
Down into the face sweet and fair
And then as the demon possessed him,
He grasped at the back of a chair

A moment, a second, ‘twas over;
The work of a fiend was complete
And poor little innocent Blossom
Lay trembling and crushed at his feet.

Then swift as the light came his reason
And showed him the deed had done
With a groan that the devil might pity
He lifted her quivering form

He pressed her pale face to his bosom
He lifted her fair golden head
A moment the baby’s lips trembled
And then little Blossom was dead.

Then in came the law so majestic
And said for this deed you must pay
For only a fiend or a madman
Would murder his child in this way

But the man who had sold him the poison
That made him a demon from hell
Why, he must be loved and respected
For he has a license to sell

God pity the women and children
Who are under the Juggernaut Rum
And hasten the day when against it
Neither heart, voice, nor pen shall be dumb.

THE COLD MAN

The cold man is *not* one of my grandmother's stories, but rather a tale that my daughter Rebecca made up. You'll find Rebecca's doppelganger in the story as Rachel, and little Danny is a fictional version of my son Andrew. I combined a couple of stories that my older kids came up with – the Dream-Suckers and the Cold Man – for this tale. There truly was an afternoon where Rebecca/Rachel and Andrew/Danny sat on the couch by an open window and she told him about the Cold Man. And he really was terrified by the tale for quite some time. Who knows? Maybe the Cold Man really is out there, just waiting for someone to continue his tale.

BENEATH THE BED

This is another story based in fact. The events did, to some degree, actually happen to my five-times-great grandparents. There really was a man under their bed, she really did tell her husband to keep snoring so the intruder wouldn't know they were on to him. My version deviates from the truth in two points: in the original true story, the man under the bed was an escaped slave instead of a criminal. Of course, they didn't know who was under the bed, only that someone was in their house. Still, it didn't sit right with me to write my version that way, so instead I made the man a criminal more deserving of his fate. The other point where my story differs is that in the real version, the husband shot the intruder through the bed. However, when talking about this story with my family over dinner one night, my older son, Jake, said, "Why didn't she just shoot the guy herself when she realized he was there?" So, I thought about it and figured, hey, yeah, why not? It surely seems like the kind of thing the women in my family would do.

THE CREATURE THAT DRAINS THE BLOOD FROM THE SHEEP

This was one of my favorite stories to write. The way Grandma Nan told it, this was a story that *her* teacher told the class one day when she was in school back in the 1930s. The story obviously is related to tales of chupacabra, though in Grandma's version she never used that word and my research tells me that the name *chupacabra* was not even given to this strange creature until sixty years after Grandma supposedly first heard her version of the story.

When I was a child and heard this story, the way I pictured the creature in my mind was as a sort of deformed human-canine hybrid. This is not the way most people picture chupacabra, but I went with the picture in my mind as I wrote, and I had Nina Lopez express the tiniest bit of compassion for the creature when she describes it to her class because I personally felt that compassion toward the creature when I was younger.

TWO HEADS ARE BETTER THAN ONE

This is, again, a story that my brother reminded me of. The only clear points to the story that we could recall were that a man somehow grew a second head on his shoulder, and it made him kill people. The rest I had to make up as I went along.

SAFE HOUSE

Safe House is the second story in the collection that did not actually come from my grandmother. It is instead a story which combines many real experiences from my childhood (all the memories mentioned – the good: reading books, berry picking, my grandfather carving small wooden toys, and the bad: getting my thumb smashed in the door, the outdoor light burning out, the tarantula – are true events) with a recurring fear and nightmare which plagued me for a long time. All the events did take place at my grandfather's house (this grandfather being Grandma Nan's ex-husband by the time I was born). Some things are made up, like the death of Granny (she did die at some point, but we'd lost all touch with her by then), the inheritance of the house (Granny sold the house shortly after Grandpa's death; I would certainly have loved to inherit it), and the death of my mother (she was alive during the writing and first edition, but has since passed away before the second edition).

Once the story reaches the part where the small creature appears, it has entered the realm of my nightmares. One night when we were supposed to be asleep, my brother and I crept into the living room where the adults were watching a scary show. I have discovered in recent years that the show they were watching was Tales from the Darkside, an episode called Inside the Closet. I caught one glance of the little creature that runs around in that episode and it haunted my dreams for years. I was certain that the creature lived in the creepy utility room that linked the old part of the house to the new. Google the episode and imagine you're a five-year-old hiding in a dark hallway late at night and you see that on the TV. Nightmares, indeed.

GIRL'S BEST FRIEND

Here is another story which has had many varied retellings over the years. In most versions, a girl is home alone when someone breaks in, and when her parents return to find the house ransacked, the girl, who has slept the whole time with her dog supposedly licking her hand, is either told that the dog has been locked in the basement the whole time, or discovers the dog hung by a rope in a closet. Grandma Nan's version, however, always involved a bunch of girls having a sleepover or a campout, so obviously my version had to as well. The story is often titled "Humans Can Lick, Too" but I felt that giving my story that name would give the ending away far too quickly.

CRYBABY BRIDGE

The last story in the collection is another of my own life experiences. Names, dates, events, all are true-to-life. I really was at that slumber party, we really did all those things, the parents really did try to scare us. I really was bothered by the whole thing, upset emotionally at the thought of a baby drowning but also fascinated by the story and the eeriness of both the tale and the location.

The Hills really did live down the street, too, and put on a spectacular (especially for the 1980s, when Home Haunts were not really a big thing yet) display every year. The creepiest thing of all? When we drove past their house every November 1, every scrap and shred of the Halloween display was gone. They packed and hid it all away in the dark of night after the last trick-or-treaters had come and gone. I always thought that was a good bit of Halloween magic and liked to imagine that perhaps they had some spell which made everything disappear in an instant.

FINAL THOUGHTS

I hope you've enjoyed at least some of the stories in this collection. You'll probably prefer some over others; that's okay. Some of these stories were my favorites, some were my brother's, some my mother's. Everyone has the ones they like best. If nothing else, I hope that in reading these you've maybe sat back at some point and thought, "Man! Grandma Nan was one cool lady."

If you enjoyed this book, please consider leaving a review on Goodreads, Amazon, and/or any social media you use. Good reviews are essential to the promotion of a book, and, if I'm being honest, to the starving writer's fragile ego as well.

Thank you for reading, come back again sometime. The tales my grandmother told me are timeless, and they'll be here waiting should you wish to revisit.

www.ingramcontent.com/pod-product-compliance
Lightning Source LLC
Chambersburg PA
CBHW030553310726
48979CB00011B/2140/J
* 9 7 9 8 9 8 9 3 0 1 1 6 4 *

Praise for
Tales My Grandmother Told Me

"These are tales crafted by a relatively new but genuinely gifted storyteller; one who can convey a variety of emotions quite effectively… sometimes tenderly with a velvet touch, while at other times like a cold shiver down the length of your spine in the dead of night."

-Ronald Kelly, author of *Fear* and *The Dark'un*

"Heather Daughrity's TALES MY GRANDMOTHER TOLD ME contains sixteen taut, tense, roller-coaster ride stories that are filled with endless twists and surprises. This is not your average grandma's sweet anecdotes. This is in-your-face suspense, so emotionally chilling that it will make you break out in a sweat. I highly recommend this book for even the most discerning reader."

-Jeani Rector, editor of *The Horror Zine*

"Darkness descends herein, and it is superb and macabre. It is a darkness that is clever, that is gleeful in its frights. A darkness from which there is no return. TALES MY GRANDMOTHER TOLD ME will catch you, bind you, and flay you while the firelight dims inexorably away."

-Eric J. Guignard, award-winning author and editor of
That Which Grows Wild and *Doorways To The Deadeye*

"Heather Daughrity's TALES MY GRANDMOTHER TOLD ME is a collection of tales passed down from a generation who knew, perhaps better than any of us, how to tell a good scare story. Presented with a knowing wink and a smile, herein you'll find all manner of creepy things spun to life with a zeal and vigor typical of the best campfire tale. Grandma Nan would be proud."

-Kealan Patrick Burke, Bram Stoker Award®-winning author of
Kin and *Sour Candy*